Angels and Women

J.G. Smith

Writers Club Press
San Jose New York Lincoln Shanghai

ANGELS AND WOMEN

Writers Club Press
an imprint of iUniverse, Inc.

For information address:
iUniverse, Inc.
5220 S. 16th St., Suite 200
Lincoln, NE 68512
www.iuniverse.com

ISBN: 0-595-00516-0

Printed in the United States of America

FOREWORD

There is a saying, "Truth is stranger than fiction." In some cases fiction can illuminate the truth.

A number of years ago Mrs. J. G. Smith published a novel entitled Seola. She claims to have been impelled to write it after listening to beautiful music. She made no pretense of knowledge of the Bible. Yet what she wrote was based on the understanding of certain scriptures, which made her novel interesting and exciting.

In 1924 the book entitled Angels and Women was published which was a revision of the book Seola. Since both these books are out of print and have been for many years you would be hard pressed to find a copy of either book in any condition today.

The way I came across the Angels and Women book is interesting. My wife and I had the opportunity to provide home care for an elderly woman living in Holliston Massachusetts. Our time living with her was brief due to the fact she would soon be moving out of the area. One day as we were helping her move some items around in her home she directed me to the basement and said there was a box there that I could have. I went down to the basement and came upon an odd shaped slender box that was about two feet high. I opened the box and found a dozen or so royal blue books with a gold title called Angels and Women. As far as I could tell this was the first time these books saw daylight since they were first boxed in 1924. I took the case of books home and put it on my porch, where they stayed until it was time to do some spring cleaning. Not being really interested in the subject matter at the time, I took a couple books out of the case and threw the rest of them away. Nothing like making a rare book even rarer! Eventually I got around to reading the book and was truly fascinated by it. I said to myself that if I ever had the time I would like to revise and republish the book for others to read and enjoy. That day is here; I hope you enjoy it.

What is the book about?

This book presents an insiders view, of what life might of been like, from the creation of Adam and Eve, to the great flood of Noah's Day, where the struggle between good and evil began. The principal characters in the novel are Satan, fallen angels and women. Angels are heavenly spirit messengers who were directly created by God to carry out His will and purpose in behalf of humans. There was a time when all angels were good. Then the time came when many of them allied themselves with Satan and rebelled against God and became evil or "fallen angels." The Bible story of fallen angels or evil spirits is briefly told as follows:

Lucifer, once a good spirit being, with great knowledge, authority and power, was not satisfied with his appointed privilege of oversight of the earth and the things upon it. In order to satisfy his ambitious nature for greater authority, he rebelled against his creator and lifegiver Almighty God. Not stopping there, and wanting complete control of the earth and all on it, Satan, (his new name meaning opposer) deceived the first woman Eve to follow his course of rebellion causing her to sin, thus taking on the second part of his name Devil, meaning slanderer. Adam, the first man and her husband, joined her in the transgression. They were both expelled from the Garden of Eden and sentenced to death. Adam lived on for nine hundred and thirty years, while Eve died some time before that. During that time there were born to Adam and Eve a number of children. Sixteen hundred years later, among these descendants of Adam and Eve, were Noah and his family.

God had permitted the angels, prior to the flood, to have supervision of the people on the earth. (Hebrews 2:3) These angels had power to materialize in human form and mingle among the human race. The materialized angels, called "sons of God saw the daughters of men that they were fair; and they took them as wives of all which they chose." (Genesis 6:2) A mongrel race resulted from these fallen angels with the offspring of Adam. These filled the earth with wickedness and violence. Their wickedness became so great that the Lord Jehovah brought upon the world the great deluge that destroyed this entire mongrel race.

The sons of God who succumbed to the temptations and thus became the fallen angels are alluded to as "Devas" in this book; their offspring as "Darvands."

The fallen angels or evil spirits were not destroyed in the flood, but imprisoned in the darkness of the atmosphere near the earth. Upon this point the inspired words of the Bible are: "For God spared not the angels that sinned, but cast them down to hell, and delivered them into chains of darkness, to be reserved unto judgment." (2 Peter 2:4) "And the angels which kept not their first estate, but left their own habitation, he has reserved in everlasting chains under darkness unto the judgment of the great day." (Jude 6.)

Since the flood these evil angels have had no power to materialize, yet they have had the power and exercised it, by communicating with human beings through willing victims known as spirit mediums. Thus hundreds of thousands of honest hearted people have been deceived into believing that their dead friends or relatives are alive and that the living can talk with the dead.

These angels have also used the occult to lead astray many young people. We are starting to see the horrific results of that today. What at times can start out as "innocent fun" ends up with some deadly results?

All those familiar with the Bible teaching concerning spiritism, will read this book with the utmost interest because it shows the methods employed by Satan and the wicked angels to debauch and overthrow the human race. With this information we can become better equipped to protect ourselves from these evil influences.

Jim Rizoli

Finding the Manuscript

A wonderful discovery is made!

Toiling along the Mountains of Ararat, on our way to Lake Urmia, we halted for the midday lunch and, while the guides were preparing it, reclined in the shade of the scanty foliage. As we leisurely surveyed the sterile landscape, our attention was attracted to an object quite unexpected in this desert place, a flower of surprising beauty, which hung from a broad shelf of rock opposite.

Edmund sprang forward to gather the wonderful blossom, and upon reaching the perilous incline while trying to sustain himself laid hold of the root of a decayed tree which had once grown there. His weight caused the stump to give way and slide down, carrying with it the earth which it had been imbedded, a portion of the rock and the rash intruder who had dared disturb its venerable rest.

When reassured that no injury was sustained, we turned to examine the spot from where the avalanche descended. Upon the perpendicular face of the rock, now fully exposed, was a clearly defined triangle about eight feet in altitude. A complicated figure sculptured in the center marked it the work of man. Speculation as to its character was cut short by our guide, who exclaimed: "That figure is the Phoenician Daleth! It means in our language 'This is the door.' Ah, what lies behind?"

In great excitement we went to the valley for aid; the triangular rock was removed, and proved to be the door of an artificial cave, about twelve feet square, cut in the mountain. The sides of this cave were smooth, the ceiling was arched, and in the center of the dome, among unknown sculptured characters, we perceived a cross of peculiar design.

Upon a marble slab slightly raised from the floor, a heap of dust, tattered fibre, and shreads of gold outlined two human figures lying undisturbed in their place of rest. Diadems that once crowned the heads of the sleepers had fallen to the floor, and by the side of one of the forms, where the hand had been, was a cylindrical object which we immediately secured.

Then the leader of our party spoke:

"No doubt this is one of the oldest tombs in the world. The inscriptions must antedate even those of the subterranean temples of Ellora and Elephanta. But why should we with irreverent hand disturb these venerable ashes? Let them rest, as we ourselves hope to rest until called forth in the awakening."

Without further words he ordered the door to be carefully replaced, and we left the shelving rock where again the dust of the years will gather, other seeds germinate and shoot upwards, and again a leafy veil shimmering in the wind will shut out from human eyes the mysterious Daleth of old Syria.

The relic thus obtained (doubly precious now that further spoliation was forbidden) proved to be a cylinder of purple amethyst about a foot in length and three inches in diameter. Upon one side, engraved with extraordinary delicacy, was the representation of a terrible flood, and upon the other a tree, under whose widespread branches were sitting a noble-looking man and woman with young persons grouped around them. Beneath each figure were detached inscriptions.

In removing the dust from the crystal a spring was touched, and the cylinder opened, disclosing a linen roll like those of Egypt (though incomparably finer), covered with minute characters which, under the rays of the sun, became intensely blue.

It occurred to one of our number, an enthusiastic archeologist, that this was a memorial of the great Deluge; the man might represent Japheth, the son of Noah, who, according to the Hebrew Scriptures, was the father of seven sons; the woman was his wife and the other female figures his daughters.

Upon this supposition we applied ourselves dilegently and, after the most exhaustive comparison and combination, found that the names of the men correspond with those given in the tenth chapter of Genesis; the mother's name proved to be Aloma, those of the daughters Samoula, Altitia, Apardis, Loamba and Jardel.

The mystery was unraveled, and we found ourselves in possession of the greatest archeological discovery of the twentieth century—an antediluvian memoir, the Journal of Aloma, wife of the patriarch Japheth!

Foreseeing the perishable nature of the precious document, travel was suspended, and the energies of the entire party were devoted to the work of deciphering. Under the supervision of our learned archeologist good progress was made, though, in our haste and ignorance, great freedom of translation was unavoidable, and frequently our insight into obscure passages was more or less conjecture.

It was fortunate that no delay was suffered; the delicate characters rapidly faded in the light; the tissue, hermetically sealed for so many ages, had lost its tenacity; day by day it became disintegrated in the unaccustomed atmosphere, and almost before the last pages were finished it crumbled to powder.

The beautiful but frail chest in which it had been preserved accidentally fell apart, and apart for the story which had so marvelously come into our possession, the adventure in the mountains might have vanished from memory like a dream in the morning.

Child of the Hermitage

West Bank of the Euphrates, Four Cycles After Adam, First Moon—Evening…

This day completes another year of my life; its events have made me unusually thoughtful.

Immediately after the morning sacrifice Allimades called me to the garden. His countenance, always serious, was even sad as we sat down under our favorite cypress-tree.

"Aloma, my daughter," he said, "you are no longer a child; maturing years and experience will bring to you, as to every human being, care, perplexity and sorrow. Your brother, who would have been a companion and protector, is dead; I buried him at Balonia. You are alone.

"Shut out from the world in this impenetrable forest, your life will be eventless, occupied by the routine of labor and religious duty; God grant you a tranquil mind. Fortunately you inherit my fondness for study. Having been carefully instructed in the wisdom of the sages, you will find comfort when your household duties are over, among the manuscripts of ancient lore and relics of other days which I have preserved for this purpose; but unless you should have many restless hours, and sigh for that companionship which you will never find, I earnestly advise you to commence a journal of your life, a record of the circumstances of each day and of your mental experience. This will be a diversion, and vary the monotony of your sequestered life. I have many things to communicate but not on this day, the anniversary of my marriage and of our departure from Balonia, as also of your birth."

With this he rose and retired into the shadow of the grove. His lightest wish is law with me—my wise and pious father—so this evening I took from the library a reed, linen roll, and an amethyst cylinder, his birthday gifts, and have come to my arbor study to begin the journal. Without doubt it will be a dull affair; fortunately no stranger eye will ever rest upon it.

What have I to record? The mists or fair weather, the quality of the harvest, our success or failure in dyeing and weaving, the increase of the flocks, an occasional alarm from wild beasts. Yet I am always happy; the garden abounds in fruit and flowers; we have many cattle; we ride, pleasant evenings, in a boat upon the river; at other times we listen to stories from father, or to mother's songs. "We" means, besides myself, Cheros and Aldeth, our servants. They came to this place with my parents before I was born, and are now getting aged. Cheros must soon depart. Aldeth is not so old as her husband, and will live, I trust, a long time.

There is but one thing to trouble me: mother is often unhappy and weeps. At such times father is stern and sad, Aldeth sighs, they chide my youthful gayety, and I am oppressed with gloom.

These moods of my parents are mysterious, connected, I imagine, with the remembrance of their former life, but I have never presumed to question them. Today I accidentally received an intimation confirming this supposition, but still I am perplexed. While tying the vines beneath my mother's window, I heard her say (forgetting perhaps, that I was near)—

"This is Aloma's birthday; how beautiful she is growing!"

I was greatly surprised, but still more so when my father groaned and answered: "Would to God she were deformed! Woman, why are you made so fair! O fatal, fatal gift of beauty! But for it how lovely and pure you are! The earth would not now be the theatre of unimaginable sin, nor would Satanas and his wicked peers control the affairs of men; these deceitful beings could not crush under their feet the hearts and hopes of mankind, nor you my wife, and I, your most unhappy husband, be exiled to this lonely hermitage. And another grief is added to our overburdened hearts: our child, now attaining womanhood, possesses the fatal heritage! Would to God she had died in your arms, as did her young brother."

By this time my mother was sobbing and, frightened by the violence of her grief, I silently withdrew, much agitated.

What can it mean? Why should not men and women be beautiful as the birds and flowers? Are they not all so? Alas! I have seen none but those of my own family.

I once read in an old manuscript of festivals, wars, travels, and marriages; perhaps these are connected with the misery of which my father spoke. I will ask him some day when he is instructing me.

Ha!—a serpent glanced across my feet so quickly I barely saw him. He too was beautiful but filled me with terror. Will he seek the dove's nest! I must follow…

O, my dear birds! The father and mother are gone; one little white trembler remains alone. But I have taken you as my special care, pretty dove; the serpent shall do to you no harm. These venomous beasts always come forth in the night; we must leave this place and retire to my chamber where we shall be safe.

No-I will stay, and repeat solemnly, "God alone is Almighty. Depart, Evil One!" That will be a protection.

How lovely is the grove in the twilight! The palms wave in the soft wind; the flowers exhale their odors; the insects chirp lazily; the birds are silent; the Euphrates sparkles in the fading light.

The river (now that I think of it) appears unreal tonight, not placid and calm, but agitated, and swelling upward; like a voice it seems to say "Coming, coming."

What is coming, old river? Nothing, I suppose, to Aloma who will perchance tread these lonely banks for hundreds of monotonous years.

The power of the name of God has power; the serpent stays away; but it is growing dark; now must we go within. O glorious golden hours! O smiling yellow moon, which I watch as through a silken veil! O vine and grove and river—dear silent friends, do you not give me joy of another birthday? True, I am no longer a child, yet I love you none the less; with you I am always happy. Good night!

Allimades' Story

Second Moon—First Day

A month has passed since I began my journal; nothing has happened worth recording until today when I found an opportunity to question my father. Mother went early with Aldeth to gather grapes for drying, and I had my tasks as usual in the cypress grove. When they were finished, knowing that candor would be most acceptable, I said: "O my father, on my birthday by chance I heard a conversation between yourself and mother, in which you spoke of beauty as a dangerous gift, as being the cause of a dreadful condition of the world, and of your own unhappiness. Would you kindly tell me the meaning of your words?"

An expression of deep pain crossed his features as he replied: "Perhaps the time has now come, my daughter, when it is proper to tell you what must sooner or later certainly be brought to your knowledge. It is a strange and mournful story in which there is but one light to relieve the deep shadows of sin and sorrow.

"Know, then, Aloma, that after our first parents, Adam and Eve, admitted the Deceiver to their counsels and had been driven from their happy home, sin and death became the unavoidable and dread attendants of human life. But more fatal than all other miseries of the Fall was the power of interference in human affairs which the Tempter had acquired. He constantly used and, from his evil nature, abused this power, slowly gaining possession of the hearts of men, until, grown bold by success, he enticed other Star-spirits from their allegiance to the Almighty, promising to establish them as great princes in the world.

"By some subtle process of which our most learned sages are ignorant, these angels changed themselves into the likeness of men, grand, strong and beautiful. These majestic beings became enamored with the beauty of women and took to themselves many wives. A race of magnificent but frightfully depraved creatures, giants in intellect and stature, were the products of these unnatural marriages, and they, with despotic cruelty, aided their fathers in the subversion of the world. The story of the crimes and abominations which prevailed would be too shocking for your ears. The worshippers of God struggled in vain to stem the tide of diabolical iniquity. Those who resisted the dictatorial will of these Devas or the Darvands their children, were disabled or put to death.

"Satanas, the most powerful of the incarnate angels, established his court at Balonia, City of the Sun, where the learning and wealth of the world were concentrated. Upon this city he lavished his immense resources. Its glory was past description; its towers, palaces, and battlements glittered with gold and gems; its pomp and pageantry excelled everything previously known. But while feasting and seraphic music filled the royal saloons, deeds of awful violence made the subterranean vaults to shudder. Yet glory be to the All-Powerful, for the fulfillment of the decrees, Lamech and Alladis, my parents, were preserved, and near this city of supreme glory and guilt I was reared in the ways of righteousness.

Being devoted to the acquisition of learning, I was spoken of as 'Allimades, the Sage of Balonia!'

"I had one brother; his name was Noah. I do not know if he still lives. He was upright and courageous, and being gifted with extraordinary powers of speech, he fearlessly denounced the foul living of the Evil Ones, and called upon God for deliverance. How often have I listened with awe, when like a torrent his sublime words were poured out in warning, and have trembled with fear of the Devas' vengeance. But he seemed to bear a charmed life; his hearers were spellbound while he was addressing them, and all plots for his assassination failed. I know now that God set a hedge about them.

"Our parents died early and we, with our few servants, were left in the world sole worshippers of the true God. To dispel his grief, my brother journeyed to a distant country in the North and there, high among the dark stony mountains, where bleak winds destroy all but a scanty vegetation, he found a noble family who had retreated there to escape the wickedness of the world. He resided in the land many months and eventually the oldest daughter was given him in marriage, and he returned to Balonia, bringing with his wife a young girl whose parents had died in that distant land. She was a lovely child, and with advancing years grew into the perfection of womanhood. Her name was Samoula.

"Noah's heart was comforted, and I still found consolation in studying works of a purer nature.

"Soon after this change in our family a shocking event occurred in the city, which drew from my impetuous brother a violent expression of indignation. Fearing that he might fall a victim to his rashness, notwithstanding his former deliverance, I tried to reason with him, but he did not listen to my caution.

"One evening, after he had with unusual eloquence addressed a great assemblage, I remained upon the mountain and conversed with him until the pale moon rose over the marble city. I spoke of the desperate condition of the world, its entire subversion by the Evil Ones. For myself I feared nothing, my unobtrusive life exempted me from suspicion or attack; but I made known to him his danger, and pleaded with, to be more moderate in his attempts at reformation. I took his hand, and well I remember my closing words:

"O my brother, I believe as firmly as yourself that God is more powerful than Satanas; many years have rolled away since the giant offspring of these detestable marriages have defiled the earth with unnatural crime! We are powerless, dear brother; God has forgotten the world!'

"He was so long silent that I looked up in alarm, for the hand which I held in mind had grown stony cold. In the gathering gloom I saw his face beam with a heavenly radiance. His eyes, dilated by strange emotion, were fixed upon the northern sky; his hand was raised, the whole attitude that of rigid attention, as if he were trying to catch some distant sound. He was evidently unconscious of my presence, and though much alarmed, I dared not disturb him. After remaining in this rapt posture a few moments, he signed heavily, his hands fell, his head was bowed, and he whispered, 'Even so, O God most mighty!'

"Presently, turning toward me, he said, without any allusion to our previous discourse, 'Allimades, three times the voice has spoken, and I know that the vision is true. Did you hear the voice, my brother?' I answered, 'No I did not. He continued: 'There is tumult in the North, the region of the mighty winds. At first like the tremor of leaves in a breeze, it increases to a gale, it crashes like a tornado; the thunder bellows, the earth quakes, the sea roars, its waters surge and swell, an awful night with blackest tempest enshrouds the world. But, above the crash and convulsion of the elements I hear a Voice, clear and low, though so terrible—it is the voice of God. I know not the words, but the same meaning always is given: "The end of all flesh is come; for the earth is filled with violence through them. Behold, I will destroy them with everything upon the earth. But with you I will establish My covenant, and will save you and your family. Build a boat, wide and commodious; it shall be your refuge when the floods of water overwhelm the guilty world."

"'I am called, my brother, and must do a prophet's work. Over me the Evil Ones have no power; God has appointed bounds which they cannot pass. But you are in danger; you must leave, though not alone, unless grief and solitude consume you. Take for your wife the beautiful Samoula, who has long loved you well.'

I answered: 'This revelation astonishes me; I know that you are indeed a prophet. The hour of doom approaches. God has not forgotten the world. I am agitated and confused; my course does not seem clear, but I will seriously consider your words.'

"As we silently descended the mountain, the hum of the illuminated city came floating toward us with a new and mournful significance, and, absorbed each in his own thoughts, we sought our quiet home.

"I was married to Samoula, and was happy in her love, but I did not leave. I lingered near Balonia where, in the great museums and libraries, I could so conveniently continue my favorite pursuits. Here your brother was born and died; his infant form lies to rest in a cave of the mountain.

"A few years I remained unmolested, for I passed in and out of the city by the most unfrequented streets, and never interfered in its affairs. I completed the copy of many valuable works, particularly those of Seth, and hopefully drifted along the stream of time.

"But upon a certain evening, when Samoula came near the outskirts of the city to accompany me in the homeward walk, a crowd of Darvands and men followed us, discussing her beauty in a way which aroused my quiet nature to furious wrath. 'Honor to the great serpent!' said one, 'we have found the queen of love.' 'What fair flesh and perfect bloom! My royal father shall have a gift at my hands,' said a towering Darvand. 'Not so fast, my brother,' answered still another giant; 'I have a better plan.'

"Terrified and enraged, I fled as fast as I could drag the half-fainting Samoula. Darkness was rapidly coming on, and hoping to elude our pursuers, I doubled back on the narrow paths and winding ways; for well I knew if we approached our home directly, fire and steel would in a few moments finish their wicked designs. As the darkness increased, one and another of the men became discouraged and turned back, until the last pursuer disappeared.

"Trembling and exhausted, we reached the dwelling, where, to our surprise, my brother awaited us. With the aid of our servants, he administered to our necessities, and when we were sufficiently restored to look calmly at our perilous position, he spoke. 'You remember, my brother, the evening of the third vision, when we sat together upon Mount Hermon, I warned you that you must leave. My words were prophetic. Too long have you lingered near Balonia; a few hours only are left for your escape.

'Satanas is already informed of the exceeding beauty of Samoula; for among women there is none so fair. With tomorrow's dawn his emissaries are to begin the search, which, if you remain, will terminate with your death, and the transfer of Samoula to the royal palace. Arise, and depart here quickly. Do not look not back until you reach the Hermitage on the banks of the Upper Euphrates, known only to us and our father. There, in the seclusion of the vast forest, you must hide from all eyes except those of the Omniscient.'

"There was no further delay. Our household stores were loaded upon the beasts of burden, Samoula and Aldeth placed upon the camels, and driving a small herd of cattle, we soon reached a narrow passage in the mountain which shut the city forever from our gaze. Here my brother, who had thus far accompanied us on a fleet horse, dismounted, and embracing me, with many tears, bade me a last farewell. 'We shall meet no more in this world,' said Noah. 'I see before me a black ,wide gulf, but I have no fear, though the earth be swallowed up and the heavens consumed. We shall meet again in peace. Allimades, you and I alone are left, worshipers of God; He will not forget us.'

"Then giving me the rein of his fleet steed, he motioned that I should mount and press onward, and from that moment I saw him no more." Here my father paused and gave himself up for a few moments to absorbing melancholy. He then resumed:

"Before dawn we were several miles from Balonia, and did not rest until we had entered the dense forest that goes on for six days' journey to the western shore of the upper river. We there refreshed ourselves, and offered the sacrifice of a young heifer.

"Having received the token of acceptance by fire from heaven, consuming the sacrificial offering, we on the following day resumed our journey with more courage, plunging deeper into the forest, and after four days' journey we reached the Hermitage, which Lamech had prepared in the hour of inspiration.

"Here we lived in safety; our garden has flourished like Eden of old; the flocks and herds have increased; and you, my beloved child, our most precious possession, were sent to cheer the solitude. In calm tranquillity have I passed the rolling years, giving you counsel or instruction, and increasing that treasury of ancient lore here, to be concealed from your innocent eyes, but which you may now persue with advantage. Within it is contained the record of families and nations, with many a story from the lives of those who have preceded us in this world of hope and fear, of pain and pleasure. You will there also find a description of the great kingdom of Satanas (to which God grant you may ever remain a stranger), and of other people and of countries in distant parts of the earth, where safe from the Evil Ones, we might have hoped to dwell, but for the stern injunctions of the prophet that we must remain concealed; discovery will be fatal.

"I am content, but your mother, now that you are grown and do not require her maternal care, is often unhappy. She feels vaguely the loss of that life in which she is fitted to shine, where she would have been the admiration of all eyes. I observe her growing uneasiness with extreme anxiety. I know not what it portends. Guard your own heart, and assist me, my dear child, to divert your mother, from any evil thoughts that would enter her mind."

The Discovery

At this moment my mother appeared coming down the avenue. She was very tired, and I for the first time, realized her exceeding loveliness. She was now in the full maturity of her charms, and of perfectly developed proportions. Her large blue eyes drooped with a sad expression; her features were of faultless symmetry; her bosom, shoulders, and arms beautifully rounded; and her color faint and delicate as that of the shells we sometimes find in the drift of the river; but the crowning glory of her stately figure was the wonderful hair. It was of a light golden color, and if extended to its full length, swept to her feet, and enwrapped her form. It hung in heavy waves, curling at the ends, and when for convenience she coiled it at the back of her head, it fell from her shoulders likes the plumes of a bird.

How graceful was her step, how firm and free! My father, with admiration and love in his eyes, arose and led her to a seat by his side. "How fares the grape-harvest, Samoula?" said he. "My lord," she replied, "the light shone into the vineyard too warmly and I left the place to be sheltered by your side." Allimades turned inquiringly, for there was more in her words than met the ear. He was about to give utterance to some thought that oppressed him when a sudden flash and illumination which dazzled us and took our breath, checked his reply.

Glancing upward, we beheld directly overhead, in an opening between the cypress tops, some object passing swiftly, and heard a peculiar sound of exultation ring out above the forest. I looked at my father in amazed inquiry. His face was ashy pale; he trembled, and fixed an earnest gaze upon the canopy above. Breathless, he cried, "The Devas!" and then, with terror depicted in every lineament, drew us within his arms and hurried toward our home, round which interwoven boughs of gigantic trees and vines had formed a perfect screen. To the innermost chamber of this secluded dwelling we retreated, and making secure every avenue of approach, my father went out to confer with Cheros. After many hours he returned, looking pale and fatigued, but spoke with composure:

"From the earliest generation it has been considered a sacred duty that every human being should, once during life, make a pilgrimage to the site of ancient Eden, and in that place of saddest memory offer prayer and sacrifice. I fear I have incurred the displeasure of the Almighty by deferring this rite. Therefore, Samoula, can you with the help of Aldeth and Aloma, prepare necessary food, also awnings to screen us from the heat of the day and the mists of night. Cheros and I will make ready the boat, and at daybreak tomorrow we will go forth upon the pilgrimage."

The unusual excitement in our household and the anticipation of a journey make me almost wild with joy. I can barely compose myself to write; but I must finish the journal, there will be so much to record after my return. Four days of travel through a strange country, the wonders of ruined Eden, perhaps the sight of human beings, ourselves unseen of them. Why should the others look so serious? There comes a premonition of change. The serpent crossed my feet—a bad omen. The river whispers, "Danger is coming!" I must beware.

CHANGE

Second Moon

O time of grief and loss! O days and O nights of woe! O dumb and lifeless hours! Is this the happy valley where my youth was passed? I seem aged now. The cypresses are black like funeral yews; their shade is darkness, and yet the light of day is hateful to my eyes, dim with weeping. O that I could find the grave! My mother mourns, but not with deep sorrow. In her soft eyes is no retrospective glance, but a gentle light like coming day.

How shall I continue the broken thread of my story? How do I make up the calendar of my life marked with so much sorrow? Yet this journal, lightly begun at the suggestion of my beloved father, must be continued as a sacred duty.

As we stepped upon the boat made ready to receive us, Father and Cheros, with long poles, pushed from the shore and aided the wide-spread sail that propelled us slowly along. The great branch of the Euphrates which we were ascending, though now deserted and lonely, in far-gone years was lively with the boats of pilgrims to Eden, and heavy vessels bearing the products of other lands to the great cities on its shore; but the Wicked Ones who control the affairs of the world have desolated this plain, striving to obliterate from the memory of mankind every reminiscence of the lost Paradise!

I was too much occupied with the unaccustomed scene to find room for mournful thoughts. Only when my eyes fell upon the snow-white lamb resting by the green herbs provided for his food, and I observed the grave faces of my parents, did I remember the strange event of yesterday and realize the serious object of our journey. As the hours of this delightful day drew to a close, and the declining sun veiled in mist warned us of the necessity for rest, Father and Cheros steered the boat into a shady cove, and made it fast for the night. We lingered long over supper, spread upon the deck of our little vessel, and when it was finished, tired with the day's journey, I lay down and fell asleep listening to the voices of my parents as they chanted the evening orison.

Before our boat was unmoored in the morning we went ashore to view the ruins of an ancient city, once famous for its magnificence and learning, now only a mound of ashes overgrown with a straggling forest. Seth, the founder of this city, was a great sage, the inventor of the characters used in writing. He caused two wonderful pillars to be erected upon which was inscribed the history of the world. These previous memorials of better days were destroyed by order of the Devas, but not until scribes of our family had copied some portions of the writings.

The scene grew wilder and more dreary after we resumed our journey; the banks were tangled with luxuriant shrubs and vines; birds of brilliant plumage flitted among the trees; bright lizards and spotted serpents darted in and out or lay coiled around their trunks.

When night came on and the journey drew to a close the river became narrower and tall trees, arching over our heads, made the way solemn and gloomy. We grew depressed and conversation died. As the red sun, like a subdued fire, sank out of sight behind the great forest, we approached a rock which rose in the middle of the river.

"Here," said my father, "our journey terminates. Upon this rock, which parts the stream as it issued out of the Garden, once stood the vigilant angelic guard with sword of flame. Alas! the way of access to the Tree of Life was completely closed to a wicked world; but man will yet eat of its life-giving leaves in the Garden of God which is to be restored in the distant future, when God's time shall have come.

"The cherub, though no longer visible, still continues to fulfill the high commands of the Eternal! Just beyond this frowning protector lies the gateway of a ruined Paradise. None dare attempt now to force an entrance, or to seek in its pure air the lost joys of innocence.

"Here we must offer our sacrifice, the last which will ever ascend from this place. I feel a melancholy pleasure in the thought. The future is dark to my vision; beyond tomorrow's light stretches an impenetrable veil; the hand of God has lowered it and I have no fear."

My father's voice grew unreal, a far-off look came into his eyes; a sigh, such as had become habitual with him, heaved his bosom; unconscious of our presence, he whispered:

"Ah, my brother, does not the hour draw near?"

THE FORSAKEN EDEN

At early dawn we were active with preparation for the solemn rite. Upon the rock was built an altar; the offerings were placed thereon. As I climbed the pathway to cover the sacrifice with lilies gathered at the water's edge, the scene beyond filled me with astonishment.

A vast expanse lay stretched before us, bounded by mountains, rosy and purple in the morning light. Born in these far-off heights, fed by springs and rills, four great rivers, widening as they advanced, rolled through a broad extended plain. Here were calm lakes and valleys, and the verdure of meadow and grove. But no flocks layed upon the grassy banks, nor cattle browsed the rank savannas, nor lion lifted his voice in the dark glen. No harvester reaped the nodding corn, or loaded with purple grapes the creaking wagon. The crimson apples lay in heaps, the nuts dropped noiselessly on the sod, the empty stubble rustled in the wind, the untouched orange and fig, decaying on the ground, went back into the parent stem to bloom again and again in vernal beauty.

Sound there was none, but sighing of the winds as they swept mournfully across the lonely Eden; no motion save that of light and shadow flitting over tenantless plains. Silence and solitude forever brooded there. A belt of funeral yews, under-grown with a thicket of brush-thorns, hedged in this land of supernal but desolate beauty. Directly in front of the Protectors Rock was a narrow opening bounded by two ancient yews of magnificent proportions; between these trees had sprung up a gigantic vine, whose wide-spread branches, twined and interwoven, made a vast impenetrable screen, closing the gate-way of the Garden of the Lord. The tangles of this deadly vine had formed themselves into spectral characters, which, facing outward, perennially renewed the inscription—"SIN, DESPAIR, DEATH"

Through a mist of tears the last look of mortal eyes was now bestowed upon the forsaken beauty of the Lost Paradise.

Omens

Turning toward the altar, my father lifted his voice in solemn confession and prayer. We then removed to the boat, and waited at a distance, repeating in the usual form our offering:

"Accept, most Holy God, the offering of your sinful but repentant creatures, and give the gracious token by fire."

A moment of breathless suspense, and the answer came but in a manner which filled us with terror. A fearful rumbling like subterranean thunder was heard; the earth shuddered; the rock heaved and with a loud explosion burst asunder. Fierce flames and sulphurous vapors rushed upward from a yawning chasm, and downward from the heavens, swallowing the altar of sacrifice and the very rock upon which we had been standing a moment before. The waters of the river bubbled, hissed, and then fell back to the old channel, our boat surged and tossed in the terrible convulsion, and the pallor of fear overspread our faces.

We turned with anxious inquiry toward father. Upon his countenance, pale as our own, was no sign of doubt or alarm. His hands were folded upon his breast, his head was bowed in resignation, and he sighed, "I accept the decree. The will of the Most High be done." Then, without further words, we hastened away from the scene of dire portent.

Aloma Receives the Gift of Prophecy

The current was now in our favor; we shot rapidly down the river, the veiled sun rode high in the heaven, and when, for the third time since our departure from home, it sank behind the western forest, we drew into the quiet cove where we had first landed. Tranquillity was in some measure restored as distance increased between ourselves and the appalling scenes of the morning, yet was the evening benediction of Allimades unusually earnest. Fatigued by the unwonted adventures of the day, all of the party, except myself, were soon wrapped in deep slumber. Cheros and Aldeth rested quietly under a palm-tree on shore, my parents reclined upon a platform raised under the tent-screen; and I lay upon a mat at their feet. The air was serene and I tranquilly rested, listening to the only sound that varied the intensity of silence-the ripple of the river as it lightly flowed past our boat.

Forgotten by the world, far from any human habitation, in the midst of a great wilderness, shrouded 'by the shadows of night, what cause was there for apprehension? Yet some unwanted agitation—a fear, or rather an expectation-rendered me for a long time wakeful, and I repeated again and again these words: "Enlighten my eyes, unless I sleep the sleep of death." Presently my thoughts became confused, and I passed into the land of forgetfulness. Did any shadow of coming evil dash across my dreams? Alas! it was the final hour of childhood, the last untroubled slumber which would seal my eyes; for before morning dawned, an event occurred which dispelled all careless fantasy, and changed forever the color and current of my existence.

I slept I know not how long, when I was startled by a flash of light, and perceived, although the moon had set, that the air was illumined by such an extraordinary brilliance that my eyes involuntarily closed again. How can I relate what followed, incredible even to myself, but which I know is only too real? I was powerless to move, and my eyes were certainly closed; but by some new and strange sight, I perceived standing directly behind me two majestic beings, in form and lineament like men, though far more stately and beautiful, but whose faces filled me with dismay.

Upon each royal brow gleamed a star luminous as their eyes, and the trailing garments were of a shape and texture I had never before seen. From the taller and grander of these figures emanated the lightning flash which had awakened me. The look of admiration he fixed upon my mother, whose transcendent beauty reflected the unnatural light, was almost as dreadful as the scowl that alternated upon his features when he turned toward my father. I was certain that they were Devas, the incarnate celestials of whose existence I had recently become aware. He who was tall and bright at length spoke in words I had never before heard, but which, by some new perception of sound, I well understood.

"More beautiful than Eve, and as true to her lord. The man must die. Prince of the West, send forth your baneful fire." The dark Deva raised his hand, and from the extended finger a slender shaft of light like a pale star-beam shot forward and quivered over my father's heart. The bright being spoke again: "Kill the girl also, Hesperus." "Not so, my Lord Satanas," said Hesperus, surveying me attentively; "this is no common maiden".

"Unlike all others," exclaimed Satanas, "clear and strong, perhaps dangerous. She must die!" "My lord, "responded Hesperus, "I have served you for some time now; and have asked no favor, but now I would like to save this maiden," hesitating a moment "for myself."

"The Star of Evening would be reflected in beautiful eyes at last," said Satanas, turning upon him a smile of surprise and triumph.

I shivered, but there was no motion; I groaned, but I heard not my own voice. I lay as in the deepest sleep until the morning sun shone upon our little boat and a shriek from Samoula aroused me. She was trying to raise my father, and loudly entreating him to speak. Our old servants awoke and came hurriedly forward, but all help was in vain. Allimades was dead.

In our distress and confusion we knew not what to do; our piteous cries rent the air. At that moment two grand looking persons came to the water's edge and kindly offered their assistance. They seemed to be men, but by the newly acquired sense I knew that the name of one was Satanas and of the other Hesperus. Samoula, too much distracted to observe my whispered caution willingly yielded to their seeming kindness, the body of Allimades was covered with a sail-cloth, and we floated homeward, hurried along by the current of the stream. Our new acquaintances told my mother that her husband had died of a sudden and fatal disease peculiar to that locality; it was a miracle we were not all dead; she must submit to the inevitable; they would convey us to our home and render all the aid and consolation in their power.

After a few melancholy hours we reached the Hermitage and moored the boat at the foot of the cypress avenue. I was filled with indignant grief when he, called Satanas, with tender affection, aided my mother and devoted himself to her care, while the wicked Hesperus conveyed the body of his murdered victim to a closely screened cottage in a remote part of the garden. Here Cheros cut down some tall trees, and despite my protestations and his own grief, covered my dead father, deep beneath the heavy cypresses, shut out from the sunlight and my loving eyes forever.

I fled to my little room, and now, hidden within it, as the shadows of night come on, how gladly would I lie down and wake no more! Oh! Is not this a dream, a delusion? But yesterday my father looked on me so kindly, his voice was sweet as he gave wise counsel or related stories of the times past. His hand was strong and warm as he aided my weak attempts to climb the rock of sacrifice. Now his eyes are without light, his face is stony; he answers not when I implore him; his cold hands lie motionless, though the trees weigh heavily upon his breast; he regards not my mother as she sits weeping by the side of the haughty Satanas.

O strange, inexplicable Death! I walk as in a dream. Stay, sweet vision, your words I do not comprehend. I catch the gleam.

Alas! my life is changed; and yet the moon rises as of old, the winds play idly with the cypress branches, all unconscious or careless of the fearful mystery in the arbor; and the voice of the river, as in the days gone by, breathes through the soft night air the same strange words: "Coming, coming, coming!"

Disaster

Seven days have passed since last I wrote, bringing other alarming events. I once longed for change and adventure. God forgive my childish folly!

I left my chamber on the morning after the dreadful day, with heavy heart and a vague sense of disquiet and danger; my mother came forward, embraced me with much affection, and for a few moments we wept in each other's arms. Sensible of a flash of light across my tired eyes, I raised them and saw the Lord Satanas, magnificent and haughty, standing near with a look of impatience, as if the scene displeased him; the Devas had not left the Hermitage. Not wishing to intrude our grief upon strangers, I hastily withdrew to the arbor study, hoping to remain unobserved; but the dark Hesperus followed me, saying—

"Aloma, I rejoice to behold your beauty, yet your eyes are dim with weeping. Let not grief overpower you; time will soothe this sorrow and the days again be bright." These words shocked and pained me, and when he extended to me his hand—the hand that had slain my father—I recoiled with sudden horror. "Forgive" he said in deprecating tones; "I cannot pardon myself if I frighten or offend you. Farewell!"

Satanas was preparing to depart. Taking the hand of my mother, Samoula, as she acknowledged her obligation for his kindness, the proud lord replied: "We would lightly esteem all service rendered to one so unhappy and so fair. Command us ever." The look which accompanied these words was bold and passionate, but her eyes downcast comprehended not the meaning.

After our new acquaintances left us, with the sense of relief came also that of desolation. Death has extinguished the light of our household; the desire of our eyes is taken; we are left alone in an almost impenetrable forest; our servants are aged; a doubtful future is before us. Yet miserable as solitude must be, an introduction to the great world is far more to be dreaded. I often discuss our prospects with my mother, but her natural reluctance is increased by misfortune, and I seldom obtain a confidential response.

Aldeth shares my dismal forebodings. One day, soon after the departure of the Devas, she led me to the grape-arbor and thus addressed me: "Aloma, I am alarmed for Cheros. Since the death of your father he is greatly changed. He hardly eats or sleeps; his life seems departing. He says nothing but, 'O my poor master! O my God!' He is old now; I fear he will die; and I have still more terrible fears.

"Our strange visitors, I love them not. It is many years since we left Balonia, and since I saw the transformed sons of God. But, dear child, I fear that the beings who have found the Hermitage are not men. Your mother, fairest of women, was concealed from the eyes of the Devas in this wilderness; she has been discovered, and we are safe no longer."

She clasped me in her aged arms, and exclaimed with deep emotion—"And you, poor child, are like your mother. God save you!" To which I devoutly added—"Save me from sin, O God!"

Third Moon

The time has passed heavily; we bleached and prepared for spinning the store of flax, gathered the hemp, clipped the hair of the camels and wool of the sheep to make fabrics, and many an hour I spent in learning from my patient mother the art of dyeing thread, and weaving the fine linen of which our garments are fashioned. The monotony of the dreary days was relieved by light labor in the garden, drying grapes, dates, and sweet herbs. We conversed little, except upon the subject of our daily occupations.

Our life went on in a dull, eventless round, until yesterday at midsun when Aldeth rushed into our apartments, exclaiming: "Cheros has disappeared! He was gathering dates upon the river bank, when a sudden flash of light and a loud rolling sound burst from the calm sky! I saw him fall, and flew to his assistance; the camels and kind in great fright were running around the place where he had fallen, but I could not find him. O my child! Where is he, where is my husband?"

We went forth in a hurry to the river. A half-filled basket was standing under the date tree; the cattle bellowed, and with heads erect looked down the stream. Upon its hurrying waters we perceived the mantle of our good old servant floating out of sight. The we lifted up our voices and wept, threw dust upon our heads, and in grief and despair sat upon the earth, while the dew and darkness fell around us.

COURTING OF THE STAR-SPIRITS

As day began to dawn, a boat was seen coming down the stream, and from the unusual light that pervaded the water, and a sudden illumination as it neared the shore, I recognized with a sinking heart the presence of the Star-spirits.

Perceiving our group, the boat drew to the landing. Two well-remembered forms advanced to the spot where we were sitting, and Lord Satanas spoke: "As we were passing by the shore, we were reminded of our last sorrowful visit, and turned aside to inquire how fares the lovely Samoula." Then surveying the group earnestly, with hypocritical surprise, he exclaimed: "Ah! what new calamity has befallen you, most beautiful of women? Why is that glorious head defiled with ashes, which should be crowned with flowers, no, with a royal diadem?"

"O, my lord," Samoula answered, "Cheros is dead! The decrees of fate are against us." "O fairest of earth's daughters," said he, extending his hands to aid her, "even fate relents in the presence of your tears. You shall be protected. Arise; forget your sorrow while we take counsel with regard to the future."

I had no time to object, for Hesperus immediately addressed me: "And you will need a friend, Aloma. Turn not away, but consider my words. Samoula will depart with Satanas; if you remain alone in this wilderness, death will soon ensue and your fair form become a prey to savage beasts. Come with me to Balonia, for here greater danger threatens. But if I may claim the sacred right of protection, safety and happiness are assured. Aloma, you have power never before conferred upon a mortal maid; you are inspired by ambition lofty as that which animates my own spirit. You were born to be an angel's bride. Become the partner of Hesperus, share in his glory, and the unimaginable fervor of an angel's passion will enkindle your human soul. Love and honor shall be mine, such as woman has never known; the treasures of earth will be laid at your feet; a princess shall you reign in my kingdom and in my heart.

"But unless the breath of a wicked world should dim the lustre of my precious pearl, I have prepared a paradise in the far West, remote from the haunts of men. No evil can encroach upon its joy, nor Deva's glance intrude upon its privacy. Above is the benignant sky, and in cool recesses flowers distill perfume; doves nestle in overhanging boughs; in the fountain white swans sail; and on the margin lilies nod. There is where Aloma will retire if the grandeur of royalty becomes oppressive."

Then my soul became enlarged, and I replied: "O Hesperus! though I am a weak and ignorant maiden, humblest of the daughters of men, by some power I can neither explain to another or myself, I know that you are a Star-spirit, made for purity and glory, but now only less wicked than the proud being who walks by my mother's side. I know that a crisis impends in the affairs of earth, a darkness hangs over the kingdom of the Devas; the day of reckoning draws close, and all who are found at that dread moment in the service of Satanas will sink to darkness and despair. I am permitted to warn you; more than that I cannot do. Be your bride? Share your power and glory? Sooner would I die by lingering starvation; sooner would I give my body to wild beasts or devouring flames. I fear not but my eternal death which would mean eternal oblivion. Ambitious? In that you said truly, but my ambitions rise beyond the present bounds of sense!"

I was astonished at my own earnestness, and hid my blushing face; but marvelously sustained, I walked away from Hesperus, who, overcome by the conflict of disappointed passions, became deadly pale and remained motionless. The Devas soon left us. I do not know what passed between Satanas and my mother. She was thoughtful and restless, but did not speak, and upon myself parental respect imposed reluctant silence. An impassable barrier seemed to have arisen between us; confidence was at an end.

* * * *

From this time on various afflictions assailed us. Many of our cattle died; trees were set on fire; the date-bearing palms were thrown down; the river rose and flooded the garden; destruction raged over the Hermitage. Our food and garments became mildewed; we drew near the gates of death. I could not but connect these misfortunes with the power of the Devas, who I knew were malignant, as they were grand and beautiful.

One memorable evening, after a day of gloom and disaster, a sudden light pervaded the scene—a peculiar brilliance which I but too well understood. Like the glitter of stars, Satanas and Hesperus appeared before us; their voices were sweet and their words gentle. Following them was a troop of strange looking beings, men of low foreheads, beardless, giants in stature, and of great strength. I instinctively recognized them as the Darvands, the sons of the Devas. They bore upon their backs large bundles wrapped in oilskins. Carefully unrolling these, they knelt and placed at my mother's feet baskets of fruit, meats, unlike any we had known. Some of the packages contained beautiful fabrics, shawls and girdles rich with embroidery, and most ravishing to my unaccustomed eyes—jewels of crystal and gold.

But curious admiration was checked when I discovered upon every package a uniform mark, in shape of a winged serpent. I looked at the bearers of the treasures. Upon the breast of the tunics they wore, and upon the band which crossed their foreheads, was the same emblem. I knew the deadly meaning of the seal. It was the form in which the Tempter appeared to our mother Eve, and I fled to my own apartment in great alarm.

Here, in the quiet of my room, the anxious tumult in my breast was soon calmed. All nature seemed to bend over me with a smile and blessing as I looked out my window upon the calm earth and sky. I was alone, indeed, without human companionship, but I recalled the omnipotence of the God of my father and feeling certain of his continued protection, the feeling of loneliness departed.

A light step at the door interrupted my meditation, and Samoula entered the chamber. "The banquet is prepared. Will you not join us, Aloma?" The question did not harmonize with my mood, and I answered, perhaps too briefly, "No, my mother."

"Our life is so sad and dull, will you not aid to brighten it?"

"I cannot, my mother."

"The Lord Satanas honors you with an invitation. Will you not accept it? Hesperus inquires for you, and anxiously awaits your coming. Will you not see him?"

Then I fell upon my knees and clasped Samoula's hand. "Dear mother," I exclaimed, "God has enlightened my mind, therefore permit me to speak. Satanas and Hesperus are treacherous friends. They have destroyed Allimades and Cheros, and can easily take our lives. But over our eternal destiny they have no power, except as it is conferred by our own will. Resist these wicked demons and they are powerless. For their wicked purpose the Devas desire possession both of the mind and of the body. Therefore they condescend to temporize, to persuade, to allure. O mother, do not yield, unless you embrace death!"

"Aloma," she answered soothingly, "you are a child, utterly without knowledge of the world. Your judgment is immature; a timid fancy has misled you. In this wilderness death is indeed inevitable. In Balonia, my early home, whether my heart has ever turned, we shall find, under the protection of its powerful lord, not only life, but happiness. Lay aside these unseasonable fears, and come with me to the banquet."

I answered—"No, my mother."

With a sigh Samoula retired; and when I had partaken of the simple food Aldeth brought for my meal I commended myself to God, and afterward slept in peace, though at intervals during the night I was awakened by unusual noises in the forest-the crash of failing trees and the sound of mechanical implements.

My first consciousness in the morning was regretting that I had left my mother and Aldeth so long alone with our dangerous guests. Robed more closely than usual, with a fold of linen over my head, I opened the door of my room, and saw at the farther extremity of the avenue the majestic form of Satanas standing before Samoula, who sat with her face averted from his gaze.

As I slowly walked toward them, I observed, more perfectly than ever, the magnificent proportions of the Deva—the massive head crowned with golden curls, the powerful shoulders and shapely limbs, the grace and harmony of every motion, the strength and elasticity of the figure, scarcely concealed by folds of a cerulean robe thickly set with silver stars.

Did my eyes deceive me? Upon his shoulders appeared something like transparent wings, which vanished into the flowing drapery. No doubt this was a son of God—he who had once been a Light-bearer, a son of the morning of creation. With quickened sense I could distinguish every word. "Let me persuade you," he was saying, "I have now held possession of the earth for many centuries and am still unconquered, yes, stronger and more secure than of old; for Heaven abandons the strife. Satanas will reign in perennial manhood forever, but not alone. Power for his strong hand, love for his heart, he desires. Among all of mortal women I met, never, until the happy hour in which your matchless form enchained my eyes, have I met my peer. Samoula must never die, rendered immortal by our great love. The equal and companion of Satanas, she must reign through the rolling ages, queen of the earth and Bride of the Sun!"

Taking from a fold in his garment a jeweled bracelet, he clasped it upon her arm, saying, "By this token the compact is sealed." I saw the band of flashing gems, bright like coals of fire, and where it closed together were two entwined serpents. In terrified emotion I cried out—"Beware, O my mother!" Satanas turned sharply, and bestowed upon me such a look of displeasure as almost deprived me of strength. I stepped suddenly backward, and found myself in the arms of Hesperus. The tender firmness of the embrace was irresistible. A thrill responsive shot through my frame; an impulse to return the pressure almost overpowered me; but at that perilous moment caught the scornful smile of Satanas as he retreated with Samoula my mother, and I cried out—"Help me, God Almighty!"

At that word the clasping arms relaxed, the magnetic chain was dissolved. With one bound I was free, and stood confronting Hesperus. He was robed in trailing garments of royal purple, a band of gold encircled his head, where rested a pale star, and, glowing with emotion, he was as beautiful as Satanas.

My face flushed with indignation and fright, yet, though repulsed, the Deva said with patient earnestness: "Listen, Aloma. I speak to you in confidence, for you are no less discreet than fair. Satanas has had many wives, and to all, as to Samoula, he promised immortality. But when tired of his queen, he subtly persuades her, and the victim retires at the solicitation of her lord, and drinks of the amaranthine cup, and dies by a petrifying poison!

"Fear nothing," he added, seeing me shudder; "together we will defeat his craftiness. His counselor possesses the antidote for his deadly narcotic, and can aid you to save Samoula from the fate of her predecessors. But I have more to say, Aloma. Unlike Satanas, Hesperus has no roving desire. Ambition alone, not pleasure, called him from the service of the Eternal. I would have power and reign a great prince. I will be the peer of Satanas, no, his dictator. I would reign in solitary grandeur, and yet only the One Supreme is self-contained, and dwells in awful solitude.

"Sometimes I long for another self to share my bounteous life, upon whose heart my own may rest in times of trouble and weariness. The women of this world have I found weak and inferior. I turned from them in disgust until my eyes met yours, O you most regal maid! We had no companions in Heaven we could love with desire; but you, warm, palpitating child of earth, are fair to me as forms that move across the plains of Heaven, and as true. I would hold you forever and forever, brightest jewel in my crown, rarest bliss in earth or Heaven. Hesperus, the passionless, bows to one of mortal women. Accept his adoration, make him happier, exalt him with your love, my queen, Aloma!"

With a look of infinite yearning he extended his arms. I was attracted, as is steel by the magnet. My brain grew dizzy, my sight indistinct, the pleading voice became a confused sound. Then memory whispered Allimades' name, reason conquered feeling, and I replied: "Hesperus, not even the safety of my mother shall tempt me. Sin is more dreadful than death, holiness is more to be desired than glory. I am inspired with wisdom and strength beyond my own comprehension; I know that you fell from holiness when you renounced the service of the Lord of Heaven. Still lower are you debased this day. You ask my love. The gift would be fatal, the union accursed. So far, you may be restored. If I yield to your persuasion, we shall sink into everlasting destruction."

I then drew forth a small dagger, which since the visit of the Star-spirits I had always carried, and I spoke again: "I know not what moves me. I do not love you, O Hesperus, yet would I plunge this weapon into my own heart to save you from the sin of my embrace." I held the point of the dagger firmly upon my bosom, and Hesperus, after gazing upon me in astonishment, silently withdrew.

Not in vain, O Allimades, did the memory of your warning come to me! Not in vain did your heart in years gone by grow dull beneath the deadly blight! And yet—the thread of my fate is tangled with that of Hesperus.

Greater Change

Place of Light, North Tower
Fourth Moon

O Incredible change of human affairs! One month ago I was an orphan child, working hard in a lonely forest. Now I am the daughter of a queen, in a marble palace, attended by slaves, looking out from the midst of sumptuous appointments upon the splendors of the richest city in the world. Day is just breaking—the hour when we were about to commence our daily toil, that we might rest through the hot and drowsy hour of noon. But here night is turned into day, and in the glare of ten thousand lamps feasting and revelry fill up the passing hours. I have just returned from such a scene; but before sleep seals my eyes I must record the events of the last few fateful days.

After Hesperus left me in the cypress-grove, I turned away and wandered alone upon the bank of the river. It still hurried on, repeating the old sound of agitation and unrest. The whole air was filled with uneasiness. The winds rushed wildly around, the leaves bristled on the trees. A flutter and a stir, then Aldeth's voice calling from the avenue, "Come, Aloma, my child!"

As we drew near the dwelling a bewildering scene met my eye. It was so like tile picture in an ancient manuscript I had just finished reading ("The History of King Irad," most famous monarch of the Land of Nod) that I could hardly persuade myself that this was not a dream. Objects I had never seen before were easily recognized, and I gave them their appropriate names. How wonderful did everything appear to my uninitiated vision, revealed in the morning light!

Before the entrance of our dwelling stood a huge golden chariot, lined, cushioned, and canopied with a soft, shining fabric of palest blue. Yoked to the royal car were six white elephants, with harness and trappings of scarlet and gold. Mounted upon the back of each huge beast was a Darvand, robed in scarlet and holding a guiding wand in his hand. In front and rear were seen a band of similar gigantic men, clad also in scarlet, with black plumes upon their heads, and marshalled in battle array. These I knew must be another detachment of those terrible beings, of whom my father had spoken—Darvands, the offspring of angels and women. Strong and powerful were they, but the expression of their faces made me recoil, and even run for protection to the side of Satanas and Hesperus, between whom Samoula stood, never so lovely and radiant as at this moment. Descending from her head and enveloping her perfect figure was a transparent veil, through which gleamed a white robe—not of linen, but of a texture similar to the blue and silver garment of the lord Satanas, who stood haughty and impatient while he waited my coming.

"Aloma," said my mother in a displeasing tone 'will you not go with us?" Trembling with consternation, but strong in courage not my own, I replied: "Our garden is overflowed, our date-trees are destroyed, our camels and possessions have perished, my father and Cheros are dead. What choice do I have, but to go with you. God save me from sin!"

At the last words a hiss arose from the giants and a scowl overspread the features of Satanas. His hand grasped the hilt of his sword, but Hesperus stepped quickly to the front, and raising his hand significantly, said—"My lord, the maiden is mine."

"Give me one moment to prepare," I cried, "and I will accompany you."

I hurried to the study, and with the assistance of Aldeth placed in a basket the manuscripts and writing materials of Allimades, and the amethyst cylinder presented by him on my last birthday. I covered all with a web of fine linen, and gave it in charge of one of the giant servants.

For one instant I yielded to the sharp pang of separation. 'Farewell to the happy past," I cried, "farewell to the home of my heart, to forest, vine, and river, and to my father's grave—a sad farewell!"

Then I returned to the waiting group. Satanas and Samoula were already seated in the chariot. Aldeth and myself were directed to occupy an apartment on one side of the car. Hesperus took a place opposite and obedient to a command from Satanas, the gorgeous cavalcade moved forward without the slightest obstruction. This was indeed a marvel, for we were in the depths of a tangled forest. I now perceived what had caused the unusual noises of the night before. The trees had been cut down and a broad highway constructed. Over this we passed swiftly without vibration or sound.

The Darvands were arranged with precision in advance and rear, but none were permitted to approach the chariot. Silent and sullen, they ran with measured tread, subdued by fear of the royal displeasure. For some hours the scenery and surroundings were familiar: dense forest, over arching trees, and blossoms like those of the Hermitage. Presently we emerged into a vast plain, where no trees obstructed the light along our pathway. At a distance were cities glimmering in the light. In the near cornfields and vineyards laborers toiled at their tasks and looked up with stealthy glance as our train passed by.

Night was now approaching. The journey which had occupied Allimades four days had been performed by the fleet elephants in a few hours. We were drawing near Balonia. During our progress the voices of Satanas and Samoula were often heard in earnest conversation, but with sense absorbed in our new changeful surroundings, and preoccupied with conjecture as to an inscrutable future, I gave little heed to their discourse.

As I seriously meditated my mind became enlightened and many doubtful matters were made plain. When the dull pressure of sense is gone, how clear the vision! Troops fill the sky, and ghostly images walk the earth, voices are on the breeze, all nature speaks. But, gloomy or glory, accents loud or low, the faithful need have no fear.

I heard a voice, as it were the breath of wind, saying, "Fear not, little one, the Devas cannot turn aside a faithful righteous human. You have set your face to do the will of the Most High; be faithful until the end. The time is at hand."

Then was brought to mind the marvelous deliverance of my father's brother, Noah; also how the, strength of Hesperus had become weakness; and I prayed earnestly:—"God of the Prophet, please be my defense!"

Balonia

As the light of the setting sun grew dimmer and the landscape began to fade, we passed the gorge in Mount Hermon where Allimades had parted from his brother the Prophet, and I beheld with the fresh delight of a child of the wilderness, the magnificent city and valley of Balonia, seat of the empire of Satanas.

Its marble towers and palaces glittered with gold; statues and fountains gleamed white among fern-palms, spice-groves, and gardens, where falling waters sparkled even in the fading light. Along its paved streets, throngs of people and carriages were moving, and a confused hum mingled with the fragrance ascending from grove and garden. Through the midst of the city flowed a broad river, and upon its bosom boats with silken sails were gliding, while myriads of unseen bells, fitfully shaken by the evening breeze, and filled the air with sounds more musical and soothing than can be described.

Upon the mountain top was a lofty building from which all the surrounding country could be overlooked. This, I afterward learned, is called the Tower of Satanas, the place where the great monarch watches the motion of the stars, or holds consultation with his angelic confederates. At the right of this imposing edifice stood another, vastly larger and more wonderful, the glorious Palace of Light. It was built upon massive arches of stone, in shape like a star, thus enclosing a great court. Upon the long lines of wall, which formed the star-points, rose marble structures, miracles of beauty.

Toward the sunrise and sunset, and to the north and south, four lofty towers overlaid with gold aspired to reach the skies. Upon the highest of these a tall shaft was erected, and around it was entwined the monstrous image of a winged serpent. As the breeze struck its pinions, it writhed around the standard, and the scales of green and the fiery eyes glittered like those of living creatures.

Below the tower of Satanas was a fair lake wherein were floating gardens of exceeding beauty. "That place," said Aldeth with a shudder, "I well remember; it is the Lake of Sacrifice."

And now, as the royal train entered an avenue of spice-trees leading to the city, Satanas checked our advance and dismissed the Darvands, whose superhuman strength had, during the day, kept pace with the swift elephants.

To avoid their bold gaze, I turned toward the mountain, and saw upon the slope a group which at once attracted my attention. In advance was a dignified man and three younger persons, who were directing the removal of timber which had been cut from the dense groves far in the heights. The halting of the chariot gave us an opportunity to observe this party more closely.

The eldest person, evidently the father, was of a handsome, man but had a sadness about him. His flowing beard and peculiar expression caused my heart to throb with mournful memories, for I imagined I could trace a resemblance to my beloved father. Two of the young men were dark and stern, but the other was fair and stately as a palm tree. He pushed from his white brow the curling locks, and surveyed the royal train with grave curiosity until his eyes rested upon the chariot. In a moment there came into his face a flush and bright consciousness like recognition, and as we moved forward, he seemed about to follow. We passed from sight, and my cheeks burned with shame, for had I not too earnestly returned his gaze?

But why distress myself? Why care for the stranger I may never meet again, and who, perchance, forgot me before I reached the city?

The sun having entirely set, the glory died out of the scene; a chill pervaded the gray atmosphere as we passed under a grand archway in the southern wall of the palace and entered the magnificent court. Depressed as I had suddenly become, I could but marvel at the wonderful architecture. Carvings, inscriptions, and tinted images that rivaled their living models, everywhere met the eye; while through mosaic footpaths and carriage-ways pressed an expectant throng, who knelt upon the ground and hailed the monarch's arrival with shouts of adulation.

As the chariot halted before the most superb of the corner towers, where gracious courtiers stood in waiting, Satanas lifted Samoula in his arms. Together they floated rather than walked up the marble stairway, and vanished from sight in the broad illuminated hall. I followed in great bewilderment. There was no abrupt sound or motion, like retreating footsteps, only the noiseless glide of a serpent.

Through long corridors, where gilded pillars upheld the vaulted ceiling, we were escorted to apartments in the northern tower. Here every imaginable luxury awaited us, and obedient slaves stood ready to anticipate our wants. The chambers appropriated to Samoula exceed the wildest dreams of imagination. The ceiling of the principal apartment is arched, and painted to represent the star-lit sky, in which the day-star outshines all others. Transparent curtains, draped from the center of the dome, soften but do not obscure its lustre. Upon the walls are gorgeous tapestried scenes of war and the chase. Always triumphant, the magnificent form of the great monarch is seen in every posture, displaying strength and beauty.

In the small banquet-room are portrayed the revels of the most spirited and boisterous of the Devas. The figures are not pleasing, but the flowers and fruit rival those upon the tables, heaped in golden baskets.

The bedroom is like a garden of roses. There again is reproduced in art the majestic but voluptuous form of the Light-bearer, reclining beneath sheltering vines, or wandering through sequestered walks in company with one alone, whose lineaments reproduce but too faithfully Samoula's beauty.

The bath is a scalloped pearl-shell, into which flows perfumed water. Mats are spread upon jasper floors, soft and bright like a grassy lawn sprinkled with flowers. Everywhere glows the action, color and warmth of life, and a light like that of the full moon pervades the balmy air.

Fatigued by long travel and unwanted excitement, I soon took leave of my happy mother for the night, and retired to the adjoining chamber, prepared for my specific use. What a contrast to that which I had just left! The walls and ceilings were all ivory, polished and carved in leafy boughs, flowers, birds, and butterflies; long mirrors reflecting beautiful designs, and startling me with the reduplication of my own white image standing entranced and motionless. Upon the marble floor of blue and gray were mats of bleached wool and goat's hair.

Chairs and divans invited rest, and in a small recess stood a dainty table containing materials for writing. Through the high ceiling a subdued light entered, making every object intangible.

It was a dream—a dream of peace and purity and spirituality. Above the couch had been placed an inscription of frosted silver inlaid upon ivory.

"Rest, sweet soul,
In the home of thy spirit."

I should have noticed what was written on the wall. Looking more intently, I saw, what had at first escaped notice, that the character used for the word "spirit" was that implying personality.

"Rest, sweet soul,
In the home of thy Spirit."

Ah, Hesperus! your love had prepared this welcome; but the home of a Star-spirit cannot be Aloma's place of rest. Then I forgot fatigue in the sense of danger, and remained a long time absorbed in thought.

Upon one side of the chamber a tall screen of ivory lace-work stood before a broad arched door, opening upon a balcony. The air of the chamber had suddenly grown oppressive, and I went forth into the silent night.

Beneath was a garden of exceeding beauty; thickets of trees and rows of flowers interspersed over lawns where gleamed alabaster vases, marble images, and jets of water rising misty and ghostlike as they were swayed by the night wind. All was secluded and dusky, except the light from an extraordinary fountain in the midst of the garden where, instead of water, were bubbling waves of fire. As these occasionally shot upward in flame, the unnatural light penetrated to the recesses of the grove, and by the irregular flash I perceived a stately figure pacing the dim aisles, whose grand, proportions and dignified carriage could not be mistaken.

The solitary wanderer paused as if his attention were attracted. I would have retired unobserved, but in an instant he was by my side and detained me gently, saying—"Do not fear; never shall one curl of your golden hair shrink from the unwelcome touch of Hesperus. O Aloma, beautiful, beloved, look forth into the western sky! You are the brightest star of the celestial group, a star radiant and tender. There once I dwelt, happy and pure. I would return unto my ancient realm. I have seen my soul, Lily of Light, and I tire of earth, its wickedness and sin. O my adored, before I leave I beg for but one kiss, the first and last." The majestic form drooped, the haughty head bent low, the angelic voice, sweet and sad as the wind-harp, trembled. "Have pity, Aloma!"

The tenderest chords of my nature vibrated to the appeal for sympathy to the grief of such a being. He constrained me by his woe, he entranced me by the melancholy of his eyes; again I felt the strange magnetism that had so nearly overpowered me at the Hermitage, and I cried out in an agony of distracting emotion—"O God, deliver me from the power of this Spirit! Save him from himself; save him from my love! Why are the creatures of God so tempted?" Then a voice fell from Heaven, saying, "To prove to them and show God's great Power!" With that, strength returned, and I raised my head. The Deva had left me.

Then I retired to my chamber and sat in anxious fear, far into the night. At length, reassured by continued quiet, the tumult in my breast was hushed, and I composed myself to record the adventures of this fateful journey. A weight had fallen upon me, my heart is as lead, my steps falter, a discord enters life, harsh, intolerable. Yet listen, doubting Aloma; does not a soft voice whisper, "The jarring symphony, the chord of suspense, prelude the eternal harmonies"?

* * * *

The marriage, Samoula informs me, will not be celebrated for several days. Certain rites of purification are required, which with preparation of the wardrobe and decorations will cause delay. This intelligence gives me hope; events may transpire to change entirely the aspect of affairs. Ah, how much that was unlooked for has occurred since the waning of the last moon!

The Dream

I cannot rest; the gloom of this unholy place increases and overpowers me. I had fallen asleep, and at that dread hour when the Giant Constellation plunges headward into the western waters, I perceived, but not by outward sense, two gaunt and ravening ghost like figures stand by the bedside of my mother.

Upon the forehead of one was stamped Murder, and upon the other, Lust.

"She is mine." said Murder,

"We will share her," said the other.

"Agreed; we will share her when the tide turns."

"O God," I groaned, "save my deluded mother, and carry away these dreadful creatures, when the tide turns."

With that the forms slowly vanished and I awoke. The meaning of the vision is not revealed. I am perplexed, yet must I again go back to my to slumber, for trying scenes are before me.

Princess Aloma in the City of the Sun

In the morning I visited Samoula and found her surrounded by ladies of the court and artists preparing for the approaching ceremony. My presence was not required, and learning that the grand monarch and his counselor were to be absent during the day, I ventured into the halls of the Palace of Light. From the dome over the great colonnade a thousand chandeliers hung. I noted the exquisite finish and decoration of the architecture, the colored mosaic of the floor, the brilliant paintings upon the walls and sculptured reliefs of the ceiling, where are portrayed love-scenes of the incarnate spirits and beautiful women, battles between dragons and angels, triumphal processions, bands of strange captives, and representations of festivals and pageants, all the carvings tinted with the colors of life.

I saw many slaves and workmen employed as I passed a long marble gallery until I reached the eastern tower. Here, finding a curtained balcony, I went forth to enjoy the view of the city and valley which lay in that direction. The mountain slope was beautified by walks and carriage-ways, groves, arbors, and fantastic structures. The shaded avenues converged toward the palace, and were at this hour filled with happy figures and elegantly appointed vehicles passing in an ever-changing, ever-renewed stream of life and beauty; while upon the lofty eminence of the mountain the enormous serpent still twined and twisted like a thing of life. The buildings of the marble city harmonized in style with the Palace of Light. Upon the highest point of each glittered a golden star.

At a distance, near the entrance of the valley, was a singular structure, entirely unlike the others, of wood, bulky and low, without any attempted beauty of proportion, at which I wondered greatly.

And while I mused, a woman attended by a slave came through the open door near me and sat down on the opposite side of the balcony.

She was attired after the elegant but sensual style of the Palace, and though beautiful in face and figure, had a worn and melancholy expression. I greeted her respectfully, and enquired if I would disturb her by remaining. She answered that these were her apartments, and that my presence was an honor. I then questioned her with regard to the low building in the distance, so incongruous with the scene of splendor. She answered, "That is Tebah intended to float upon the great waters."

"A boat?" I exclaimed in astonishment. "It is far from the-river and much too large to float upon its surface."

"Yes," said the woman, with a smile, "that enormous boat has been for quite a time in building, the work of a fanatical old man and his sons. They believe that this valley will presently become a sea, upon which they will be securely borne during a great Flood which will soon visit the earth. They declare that the God of Heaven is displeased with the present state of the world and has determined to destroy all living beings.

"It may be true, as the old man says, that there is a God in Heaven, but Lord Satanas certainly possesses the world; all is now under his control. The princes of the earth," she added with a sigh, "have yielded to his might, and now (here her voice sank, to a whisper) none are left to oppose his majesty. So the foolish preacher has built his own tomb, which Lord Satanas will consume by lightning some day, after the old prophet and his family are ensnared within it."

Then I said I with increasing interest, "O my mistress, make known the name of the preacher!"

She answered: "He is called 'Noah, King of the Waters.' Unlike any other man of these times, he has taken but one wife. Two of his sons have followed his example. But the third, who is by far the handsomest man in Balonia, has never married or even loved. The fair ones of Balonia would sacrifice much to see him at their feet, but the toils are spread in vain."

Instantly my thought reverted to the group I had seen upon the Mountainside: the timber was for the building of Tebah; the patriarch was my father's brother, the resemblance was not accidental; the sons were my cousins; and the beautiful youth whose gaze had, I fear, found in my eyes a too responsive answer, was the youngest son, he of whom the woman spoke. Why did I tremble unless I was in error? Ignorant of my interest in the family, she changed the subject, and with listless indifference said:

"And are you not the daughter of the new queen? She is surpassingly beautiful, according to report, though mature, and may not hold sway longer than did the last favorite."

"When did—the queen die?" I inquired.

"I do not know if she is dead; it's been but a moon's quarter since she drank the amaranthine cup, and was placed in the crypt of Nirvana. It is said that Lord Satanas can recall those whom he places there, but I have been in this Palace many long years, and have seen none come back from that chamber."

Why are the queens not warned?

"All remember the fate of that rash maid Tamoulee, who, to save her beloved mistress, spoke one word of caution, to no avail. For many years sailors, drifted out of their course, have heard screams issue from the dark caves of the lone rock Zem, where still the wretched Tamoulee suffers.

"Satanas may offer to woman the cup of Nirvana, but never from love.

"Why do I dare speak this way to you? O child, truth and honor, like a halo, encircle your brow. Your eyes disarm doubt and jealousy. Yet by this trust my life is endangered! Yet what do I care? Long since I became apathetic, hopeless. Even ambition dies in this smothering atmosphere. The reflections of the pictures are bright, but the shades are midnight gloom. I know the secrets of this place too well. Would you know them? Then must your eyes be closed to the sights that you will see your hearing be dulled to the cry of pain and woe; love and pity must hold no place in your breast, and your heart must be turned to stone.

"I am reckless and tired of life, or I would not say this. Suspicion lurks in every alcove; Revenge hides behind each column; Envy and Jealousy walk the corridors; Treachery and Conspiracy scarcely conceal their malignant forms in the tapestried chambers; Torture and Murder gloat over the work of the foul fiends in the vaults below. You are beautiful. Take my advice, and secure the protection of one of these celestials; otherwise, you will not be safe for one hour. Uronion, my lord, is scribe to Hesperus the counselor, and has access to the keys of the Palace. With him have I wandered through its secret recesses, and nerved my heart against despair by witnessing woes greater than my own."

Touched by pity for this unhappy woman, I asked her name and history, and how she had become an inmate of the Palace of Light.

The Story of Minerva, the Sorceress

"My name," said the woman, "is Minerva; I was born a thousand miles from BaIonia, on the shores of the great inland sea, a land of perpetual spring, of beauty and delight. My father was a powerful prince, who governed a happy people by just and equitable laws; for he was a worshiper of God. He refused the tribute exacted by Zaradis, a fierce Deva, who intruded himself upon the earth after the descent of the Lord Satanas, and established his kingdom on the borders of the land in which for many years the dynasty of Arratas had ruled. The monarchs of our line, who were powerful and wise, remained undisturbed after the other princes of the world had succumbed to the Deva powers.

"O happy days, when in my father's royal boat, with Senaris my betrothed for a companion, we sailed across the Midland Sea and passed the narrow gate of rocks which separate it from the great waters which lie on the western edge of the world. To the far west upon the bosom of the Atlantine deep lay the Amber Isles, raised by the ocean in distant years.

"Where the light winds wafted us, and many months we remained in the land of beauty and never-failing greenery gathering gold and purple fruit, breathing health and delight from the air of the ocean, until my father was summoned to defend his kingdom from an attack of the Devas.

"Vain struggle! Zaradis made alliance with Lord Satanas. They united their armies of Darvands, strong, crafty, cruel warriors, and swept over our kingdom like fire across the stubble. Our city and palace were burned, the army slaughtered, and my father, his generals and priests, were tortured. Semaris, my betrothed, was slain; my mother died of a broken heart; but I was taken to the court of Zaradis, and spared on account of my beauty.

"Accursed possession, it is leaving me now!

"I should have been the queen of Zaradis but for the arrival of a still fairer captive I was not chosen. I was married to the Deva Uronion, and soon after our union, moved to Balonia, for the queen had been strangled, and he feared from certain rumors that Zaradis' fancy for me might return. Here have I lived, unhappy certainly, though with one of the most constant of the gods; for Uronion is encouraged by his master to abstinence, as he condemns the universal license.

"When I came to this place I retained the impress of my early faith, but have long since abandoned all expectation of intervention from Heaven. I have listened to tales of war and subjugation; to stories of mighty deeds accomplished by the Star-spirits; I have seen the unsparing cruelty and undisturbed domination of their giant sons, until I am convinced that faith in God is a fiction of the imagination. The weak minds of the common herd crave a religion, and Satanas has supplied it in the worship of his Symbol—the serpent.

"The kingdoms of earthly princes have passed away. God, if there be one, cares not for men, nor takes notice of their affairs. He leaves the earth to my Lords Satanas, Zaradis, Hesperus, Ramidas, Saranzia, Owadu and many others, who reign in distant regions. But all pay allegiance to Satanas, the Light-bearer, who seduced them from Heaven and placed them in subordinate power.

"No doubt you are still deluded by fantastic hope. This will soon be dissipated, and you will acknowledge that God has forsaken the earth. You will abandon the fallacy of prayer, and curse your fate and the Devas, as I do at this moment."

THE PRIESTS OF SATANAS

Astonished by such a history, and shocked at the impiety of Minerva, I hesitated to reply. Just then a procession of strange figures, passing a narrow pathway which led from the city, diverted our attention. In advance was a band of men, hideous in aspect, with scarlet feathers on their heads, upon their bodies purple tunics, emblazoned with yellow dragons, and in their hands sharp curved swords.

"The Priests!" said Minerva with a shudder.

"Who are the Priests?" I inquired.

"Debased, truth-hating, power-loving men, who attend the great serpent, and offer the sacrifice upon which he and his brood are fed every day at noon."

I cast another timid glance at the procession. Their proud, cruel and unrelenting faces occasionally turned toward a line of naked men, who tottered after them with feet hampered by heavy chains and hands bound behind their backs; their heads were bowed; their mournful wail betokened fear and despair.

"These," said Minerva, "are victims about to be slain at the Lake of Serpents, receiving punishment perchance for some slight offense to our masters, or without pretext sacrificed in malignant wantonness to satisfy the clamor of the superstitious and imbruted crowd."

Appalled at the sight of such monstrous cruelty, I arose in great fear, and hastened to the solitude of my own apartment before I should witness some other horror.

Toward evening I was aroused by the entrance of Samoula, now doubly radiant in the gorgeous robes and gems presented by her enamored lord.

"Aloma," she said, "our simple life at the Hermitage has not prepared us for the splendor and magnificence we now have at our command. This royal state confuses me; I fail to realize the proper bearing of events. Sometimes my heart misleads me, and I fear the change is evil. But these doubts are the result of ignorance and unfamiliarity with the world. The Lord Satanas is grand and noble; he excuses my deficiency and devotes himself to my happiness. He would like to exalt me to his lofty standard.

"This evening the crystal court is to be illuminated in honor of our arrival, and I am to be presented to the people of Balonia as their future queen. You are invited to share in the ceremonies of the hour. Slaves will soon place at your disposal robes of honor and jewels fit for the daughter of a queen. O my child, do not refuse to accompany me and participate in my fortune and glory! You are the only tie that binds me to the past. I may yet wish to retrace my steps; let not this link be broken."

"I will accompany you," I answered, "but let not the queen be displeased if I refuse the jewels and robes of state. The gifts of Satanas will not become the daughter of Allimades." Then I wept, and continued "O my mother, the change is nothing but evil! You will never retrace your steps."

"You are excited, and speak wildly," said Samoula. "I will leave you to calm yourself before the night comes on."

My appearance must have justified her words, for I felt the strange tremor and the supernatural power of speech and sight, which since the night of Allimades' death has often inspired me. Samoula retired, and presently came maids and eunuchs bearing the gifts of Satanas, and also a jewel box of exceeding beauty sealed with the signet of Hesperus.

After they had retired, I laid aside the royal gifts, enwrapped myself in a veil of the finest linen, transparent and white as the marvelous flower that never sees the sun, and then awaited the signal of illumination.

JAPHETH

We entered the crystal court amid a blaze of light, with sounds of ravishing music and acclamations of the throng. A band of Darvands escorted us to a high platform in the center of the court, where Satanas with royal majesty awaited the queen; and as she, in robes of more than earthly splendor, took her seat by his side, a tempest of applause from the spectators favorably shook the lofty building. I was placed in a golden chair upon a step of the stair, and for a moment gazed in awe at the magnificence of the architecture. The inner court was surmounted by a lofty crystal dome thickly hung with glittering prisms, a thousand pillars of hyacinth entwined by golden wreaths upheld the immense arch; the marble walls were made airy by delicate and graceful perforations through which the cool night breeze could penetrate.

In glancing over the happy throng, my eyes rested upon a figure standing in an open archway, which at once startled me and riveted my attention. Tall, graceful, serious, in this white-robed figure my eyes and heart recognized the youth of the mountain, whom I recognized as the youngest son of the Prophet. O could I just speak with him, one of my own kindred, a man unpolluted in the midst of universal corruption, one I could safely trust! But if this were not the young man I had seen—if Minerva had mistaken his character—if he should have no interest in my welfare, or should despise the daughter of the queen of Satanas, what then? These doubts tore at my heart, and destroyed all interest in the scene before me. I was dimly conscious, as in a confused dream witnessing the wonderful feats performed by men and wild beasts. Look at the enchantments, intoxicating odors, dancing, music and feasting, its hard to believe that I'm in the midst of it all But one thought absorbed me: shall I speak with this young stranger? Does he regard me with kindness?

The night wore, away. I remained motionless upon the step of the platform, and still in the doorway the white figure was seen.

But although I had eyes for none other, I was not myself unobserved. Eldero, a favorite son of Satanas, stood near, regarding me with bold and insolent admiration, often addressing me in language of offensive flattery. I grew alarmed, and was longing to change my position, when Hesperus, the master of ceremonies, accosted me in tones of melancholy rather than presumption. "Aloma, would you like to leave this place?"

I hesitated to reply, for, more than present discomfort, I feared his solitary escort. He seemed to divine my thought, for a deeper shadow overspread his grand features, as he gave orders to a band of slaves: "Attend the princess, and do whatever she ask."

"Ho! Ho!" said the Darvand with a sneer. Does the passionless Lord Hesperus really care about this fair maiden?

The eyes of the Deva flashed fire. He raised his hand in menace, and bestowed upon my tormentor a look so terrible that he shrank back in silence. Fearing the consequences of a moment's delay, I directed the guard to take me to the open air; I passed quickly through the throng, whose rude gaze and free remarks made the breath of night doubly welcome as we drew near an entrance to the garden.

Then it was made manifest the guiding hand of the Almighty; for it came to pass that, when the slaves attempted to reach the northern tower, a band of dancing girls entered the court, and we were pressed backward by the throng to the eastern side, where still remained the unknown youth. He respectfully stepped aside as we passed. I seated myself upon the balcony, and the cool breeze soon restored my courage.

The wonderful scene I then beheld is impressed upon my memory, ineffaceable in outline, color, and shading. The veiled moon hung low in the sky; in the east could be seen the faint flush of dawn; the palms and acacias rustled and whispered secrets of the night and of coming day. Blending with their mysterious breath were sounds of revelry in the Palace, music and the measured tread of the dancers, the harsh voices of the giants, the flattering tones of men, light, assured laughter of beautiful women, musical accents of illustrious Star-spirits, sighs of tired and panting slaves. The glare from illuminated hall and dome, shimmering through panel and archway, shone out upon obelisk, statue and fountain; it mingled strangely with the perfume of the tropical night, but did not dispel the black, ominous shadows moving noiselessly through this paradise of sin.

At the further end of the balcony stood the slaves in fixed immovability, and relieved against that dark background, in the full blaze of glory which streamed through the archway, stood the white-robed stranger like an angel of light. His earnest eyes met mine with entreaty; his hand was half extended.

A sudden sense of the supreme importance of the moment, a feeling that the golden opportunity of my life was passing away, that he would vanish in the darkness and be lost forever, overpowered all reserve. Unmindful of the exposed situation, of prying eyes around, and of the danger that might follow, after a moment of hesitation I motioned for him to approach. He came forward, and in a manner composed and respectful at once reassured me.

"Fair princess, you are Aloma, daughter of the queen. I am Japheth, son of the Prophet. Hopelessly separated are we by worldly distinctions, and yet the rapt purity of your face, the simplicity of your dress, the indifference or distaste you manifest to the pageantry within, give token that by sympathy we are not divided.

"Do you ask why I am voluntarily in scenes where you appear only by compulsion? Know, then, O beautiful stranger forgive my boldness—that I saw you in the chariot of Satanas on the evening of your entrance into Balonia, and the hope of meeting you once more led me to enter the Palace, and join an assembly whose character and amusement my soul abhors. I was afraid to speak to you, and now that I have the opportunity, with many thoughts and desires I await your favor."

Hearing this, my heart revived, and I answered—"O son of the Prophet, permit me to make known my brief history. You called my name rightly—Aloma—and I am the daughter of the queen, but my father was Allimades, the Sage of Balonia, son of Lamech and brother of Noah."

With heightened color and joy in his eyes he drew nearer, and said—"O princess, you are my cousin! You, the daughter of Allimades, my heart leaps with joy on seeing you!" Then, taking my hand, he trembled, grew pale and seemed unable to repress the low rapid words:

"Aloma, your face and voice are an inspiration, a revelation of which I have dreamed, for which I have prayed. You are the fulfillment of my heart's prophecy, the promise of Heaven. Forgive this abruptness, this emotion. I am amazed; I cannot control myself I have waited for you so long; yet now all my former years seem like a dream, and this brief moment, the waking to life and reality."

Though much affected by these words, I repressed my emotion, and answered quietly: "We are indeed related; the discovery gives me inexpressible happiness. There is much to be spoken, but the night wanes; to remain longer in this place would invite observation and danger. Even now I perceive the glance of Hesperus toward us. We must part."

But Japheth could not refrain. "Dear cousin," he said, "ask me not to leave you—rather come with me to my father's house, where among family you will find safety. You cannot realize the dangers of this glittering palace. The thin film of splendor scarcely hides its sins and crime. If you are again immersed in the tide of false glory, I fear you will be lost from me forever, as your image has faded from my longing sight in insubstantial dreams. Nothing but a miracle can save you in this accursed place."

Again my mind was suddenly illuminated, and the purpose of the Most High revealed. The gift of prophecy was bestowed for my own salvation and that of others; and I answered confidently—"The miracle has been performed. I am possessed of a power more potent than the deception and violence of Deva or Darvand. We shall meet again."

At this moment there was a tumult in the court, and a herald's voice announced the retirement of the queen. I motioned Japheth to leave me. He vaulted lightly over the railing of the balcony, and in a moment was lost in the darkness below. I gave the order to the slaves, and they moved toward the northern tower. As I passed the son of Satanas, his bold eyes saluted me, and he muttered—"the princess is fairer then the queen; her step outgraces even the dancing of Oradel. Where were my father's eyes when he preferred the mother? I swear this is a morsel fit for a god! The Deva opposed me, but if he does not want the damsel, she is mine. Our lords are delicate in their courting; a Darvand does not hesitate nor relent."

His brutal expression and villainous language were terrifying. I moved quickly with the guard, and unmolested reached my chamber.

Here have I endeavored to review calmly my perilous situation and the adventure of the evening, which seemed so unreal. I could doubt my own identity, but the sacred manuscripts of my father lie before me, and in the mirrors which adorn this magnificent apartment are reflected the familiar form and dress of the Child of the Hermitage. Now will I lie down to rest, and forgetting these new conditions, wander in dreams through the cypress-groves, and listen once more to the voice of Allimades blending with the murmur of the river.

* * * *

When this journal was laid aside for the night my adventures were not over. With a sense of danger averted, and a vague foreboding of peril to come, I sought my couch. The lights in the chamber were extinguished, there was no moon in the sky, and pale starlight coming through the window made every object shadowy and undefined. A creeping chill came over me as a fresh breeze swept suddenly through the chamber. Was I dreaming?

I opened wide my eyes and perceived with horror that a large panel in the opposite wall moved inward, and the shaggy head of the wicked Eldero peered through it. In an instant he seized me with giant grip, enveloped my head in the bed-covering, and darted through the open wall, down an unfamiliar corridor, toward a staircase which I knew must lead to the vaults below. Whirled rapidly along, helpless in an iron clutch, I struggled in vain to make audible my smothered screams; for deeds of violence and cries of despair produced no impression upon dull sleepers well accustomed to such sounds. No curious eye looked forth from the silent dormitories; no vigilant watchman raised his hand to interfere, as the Darvand fled swiftly down the darkened hall to the steep and fatal descent.

But just as I, felt myself lowered, an bright light filled the air, the arms of Eldero were wrenched asunder, and alone he was plunged headlong into the darksome pit, while the wrathful voice of Hesperus rang through the stillness of the night: "Lustful monster, insatiate ravisher, would you dissolve this pearl of Paradise in the cup of your sin?"

Again I was carried rapidly through the long corridor, back to my own apartment and placed upon the bed. Swift and sudden as his coming was the departure of the Deva. There was a profound sigh, and the displaced panel moved into its former position. A sound of closing bolts and bars followed, then silence, solitude and shade. I now felt that safety was assured, and with supreme gratitude for the marvelous deliverance, thoroughly exhausted I sank into slumber.

The Sorceress and the Prophet

I slept soundly until midday, and was then roused by a voice at the chamber door, which I recognized as that of Minerva. She called my name, and when I admitted her, she offered to assist at my dressing table. The extreme simplicity of my dress rendered such aid unnecessary, and after some hesitation she spoke again:

"Aloma, I believed that all fear of God and sympathy for my own kind were dead in this withered heart; but your innocence and purity, sweet child of the wilderness, have brought back vividly the memory of early days, when like you I was uncontaminated by the wickedness of the world, when in faith I knelt with my princely father to offer the daily sacrifice, when we mingled our tears and lamentations at the tomb of the brother beloved and early lost, when with pleasure I pondered upon the wisdom and piety of the ancient and dreamed that I might emulate their noble deeds.

"Why was I brought to this evil place, where in the pursuit of power and pleasure I have forgotten myself and God? Aloma, I love you because you are what I once was, and I abhor myself for what I have now become. You may perchance escape downfall and ruin, but how can I be restored? For the Sorceress of Balonia there is no atonement, only the dreadful end.

"But what folly has seized me that I bemoan my fate in this insane manner? Let us drink and be merry. Man dies and Pleasure flies; we must keep pace while she wings her way over banquet-halls and perfumed couches." With that, she took from her bosom a small amphora of transparent jade, and pouring out a few crystals, round and red like drops of blood, threw them into the lustral, where, according to the custom of the Palace, fragrant oils were kept burning to perfume and purify the air. As the tiny balls touched the flame, they burst with a ringing sound, and the apartment was filled by a dense mist of pungent, intoxicating fumes, in which every object was intensified, and the sorceress herself appeared the incarnation of youth and beauty. The vapors were slowly resolved into the semblance of moving figures, surrounded by all sensuous delights, while strains of voluptuous music enchanted the ear. In the midst of this bewildering scene I perceived a well-remembered Deva kneeling before my own glorified image.

My brain was dazed but, conscious that there was danger in such delight, I exerted to the utmost my fast failing will, and fled from the atmosphere of enchantment to the balcony, where, in the fresh air I soon regained full possession of my reason.

In a few moments the unnatural scene had vanished, and Minerva came to me in great agitation, saying, "For the first time Maya fails, but Homa remains; drink, fair girl; let us drink the cup of Homa—nectar of the gods, longed for by men; antidote of sorrow, balm of memory, dissipater of fear—give me a drink that I may steep my brain in forgetfulness. Where is the Homa, girl?"

Her excitement was painful as she returned and searched the apartment wildly. The Homa had complete controll over her and had mastered an awakening conscience.

With profound pity I took her hand and said: "Minerva, that for which you search is not here. The Homa and your enchantments are dangerous. They do not heal, but poison the soul. But I do have a cordial for a diseased mind. Listen, and I will tell you of this medicine. Minerva, the Devas are cruel, unrelenting, full of hate. The Almighty is compassionate, kind and forgiving and shows mercy to those who seek his forgiveness.

"But I cannot hope, and for me there is no mercy; you do not know, simple one, the extent of my wickedness. I must drink the Homa, it stupefies the brain; and yet, when its power is over, I wake to greater horror. Where can I turn? Only to death?"

After a moment of silence she exclaimed: "What day is this? The day when the Prophet warns the scoffing crowd—almost the very hour—hurry! hurry! He is wise, he is pure; no drop of Homa has passed his lips, confusing reason and weakening will. He can instruct us.

"We will go to the mountain-side; the chariot awaits my call; the name of Uronion upon its front is a passport, though all men in the kingdom of Satanas know and fear Minerva the Sorceress. Yes, to the Prophet I will go, even if it means losing my power and, my life!"

Anxious to enlighten Minerva, and also to look once more upon the face of Allimades' brother, I gladly accepted this proposal, and we were soon on our way through the city to the mountain. I was delighted with the changing scenes of the busy marts, so new and unfamiliar, the buildings of various forms and uses, the long rows of colossal images which bordered the highways as we entered the royal avenue where dwell the giant sons of Satanas.

The road was broad, so that a score of chariots could pass at once. Upon its borders were gardens of exceeding beauty, a paradise of fountains and flowers. Stately peacocks paced the white walks, birds of gorgeous plumage fitted through the shrubbery, the golden fishes darted across the crystal basins.

Beyond these gardens stood beautiful palaces, sculptured with various devises. Before every mansion stood a slender obelisk, entwined with living vines now full of scarlet blossoms. Upon the green turf were little people disporting in capricious joy. They were the first I had ever seen, and in a transport of admiration, I exclaimed: "Oh, the children, the beautifil children!"

Minerva looked upon me with surprise. "You were brought up in a forest, and have never before seen children, and yet you recognize them at once and give them their appropriate name. And so it is in all things. Without mistake you accord to new and familiar objects their proper designation. Where does this power come from?"

I answered, smiling, but somewhat puzzled: "Is it not so with every person? It was certainly so with Adam our forefather, the proper word must have occured to him, as to me, with the occasion for its use. But I am often myself surprised at this power. I do not remember to have possessed it before Allimades' death. Perhaps it is a special gift of God."

Just when we reached the heart of Balonia, and here on either side, were rows of colossal statues, the most fearful and imposing in the city, with heads far outstretched, back of which pointed forward great pinions meeting in midair. The effect of these hideous forms was freightful. I shivered as we passed into their shadow. As we emerged again, and entered the country, many people were seen going toward the mountain. We followed, and were soon in the presence of the famous Prophet and dismounting from our chariout, drew near to listen. Standing with his three sons upon a low terrace, he addressed the crowd. His face was solemn even to sadness, and the words that met our ears were these:

"Yes, for many years have I lifted up my voice in warning and entreaty. My soul has been daily vexed with your abominable deeds. You have wallowed in gluttony and drunkeness, in lust and lechery; you have said to avarice, 'You are our father,' and Sensuality, 'You are our mother.' Reckless and drunk you have embraced destruction.

"O wretched slaves of a merciless despot, your manhood is lost, your lives are forfeited; you are doomed! With strong groaning and tears, with fasting and sacrifice, have I sought the almighty on behalf of the sinful sons of Adam. Repent! Repent! before the thunders of heaven shall burst upon your guilty heads!" Then throwing up his arms he exclaimed: "O God, it is vain, all in vain! The day of wrath is at hand!

"The night wind whisper a dreadful secret. In far off regions I hear the mutterings of the approaching storm. The ominous roar of ocean as borne upon the blast; its grapes to devour its prey. The seals of Death and Sheol are broken, and Vengenance rushes forth on the wings of destruction. Too late! too late! You will hear my voice no more; the Prophet's work is ended!"

He ceased, and there was a great commotion in the crowd; but I gave no heed to it, for Minerva, shaken like a reed in the wind, cried out—"O prophet of God, I repent! Is there no mercy for me?" He heard her and was about to approach, when a malignant demon who hovered behind a black cloud swooped out of the sky, and aimed a dart at the Prophet. But a holy angel, until that moment unperceived, rose at the critical moment and with his shield turned the weapon away. At the Prophet's narrow escape I fainted and for some time was unconscious.

Presently I recovered, and found myself in the arms of my cousin, who, attracted by the cries of Minerva, had discovered me as I fell.

"You are cold and pale, beloved," said Japheth in alarm; your form is rigid and your gaze fixed; you are not going to leave me? This cannot be your death!" Then, suddenly inspired, I answered—"Not in your arms shall I yield up my parting breath. In the last hour of life I shall rest upon another breast, but one so much resembling yours O Japheth!"

"Aloma," said he with wonder, "do you, like my father, a have prophetic power?" And I replied solemnly, "God only knows."

I turned toward Minerva, and found her engaged in discourse with the Prophet, who unconscious of the attack upon his life (for his supernatural perception extends not to vision), was absorbed in giving her instruction and comfort. He did not notice my presence, nor that his son was with me. I, therefore, stepped quietly into the chariot; Minerva followed, and we turned toward the Palace.

It was late before we recrossed the city, but artificial lights made the warm night like day. The streets swarmed with a mixed multitude, men and Devas with their beautiful wives and children, all abroad to catch the breeze which at this hour sweeps down the valley. As we drove along, impious language shocked our ears, revealing discontent, jealousy, and hatred. Minerva appeared ill at ease and thoughtful. To divert her mind and inform myself, I inquired, "Why do these people continue in their bondage? Why not resist, though in the attempt they perish?"

"What can be done?" she replied. "Countless plots have been formed, conspiracies to destroy the life of Satanas, by fire and flood, by steel and poison. His body is impervious, his spirit-forged weapons irresistible. The power and grandeur of the Darvands, their very existence, depends upon the will of the Devas. Therefore they yield outward obedience, while within smolder fires of hatred and rebellion."

By this time we reached the Palace. Minerva embraced me affectionately at parting, and when I said, according to custom, "God be with you," to my surprise she added devoutly—"May it be so to the end."

As I entered my apartment, the voice of Samoula summoned me to her chamber. She was surrounded by admiring slaves and women, who were displaying for her inspection and choice, elegant costumes designed for the coronation. She asked my approval of a robe so glittering and transparent that it might have been formed of woven sunbeams, and a veil of similar texture, embroidered with minute gems that reflected the lamplight in twinkling gleams.

Totally unconscious of danger, she is absorbed in the ceremonials and magnificent preparations of which she is the brilliant center.

Satanas is rarely in the queen's apartments, being, it is remarked with some surprise, unusually occupied in affairs of state.

While the preparatory baths, oils, and cosmetics have greatly heightened Samoula's beauty, they seem to have stupefied her reason and conscience. Oh my poor deluded mother, how gladly would I again warn her of the perils by which we are surrounded! But there is no opportunity. Jealous eyes, quick ears, and ready tongues are ever near.

To this inanimate scroll will I commit my story, and entrust my fear, hoping that some gleam of maternal affection may lead her to persue this page and admit once more to her confidence the child who would cheerfully lay down her life to save her.

Third Day at Balonia

I rose at dawn of day, and calling Aldeth to accompany me, went forth to breathe the fresh air of morning. This I know would be my last opportunity to walk the streets in safety, for at noon the subordinate princes with their retinues were expected at Balonia, where they had been summoned to pay the annual tribute and take part in the ceremony of the coronation. During their stay the city will be filled with Darvands, who are without the self-repression of their spirit-fathers: the earth is filled with violence through them.

At that early hour the long corridors of the Palace were silent. The court was empty, and gave back a hollow echo to our footsteps as we passed out through the eastern gate. The city of Sin was asleep. The intriguing brain, the heart throbbing with anguish or anger, the hand of stealth, the feet swift to pursue evil, must sometimes rest, and this was the hour of tranquillity in Balonia the capital city of the gods.

Nature was also resting. Too calm and silent seemed the morning's dawn. No breeze lifted the drooping leaves; no chirp of bird or insect disturbed the brooding silence. A gray haze hung over the sleeping city, an ominous hush pervaded the valley. I paused to listen. I sat upon the earth and leaned my head upon a projecting rock. Did I feel a tremor coming from the bowels of the earth, the beginning of an unborn earthquake? I looked up into the soft sky. Could I not discern in the far—off mist the tumult that was soon to comet?

I rose and hastened on until a short turn in the pathway brought me directly in front of the building called Tebah. Here was animation. The smoke of early sacrifice slowly floated heavenward, and the Prophet with his family bowed before the altar. Greatly affected by this reminder of my former life, I stepped forward and knelt with the worshipers. The quick eye of Japheth detected the presence of strangers, and when the group arose, he came forward with words of welcome, and taking my hand respectfully, led me to his father.

"This," he said, "is the maiden of whom I spoke, the child of Allimades, who has this morning worshipped with us to the God of her father." The Prophet gazed upon me earnestly, and tears came into his eyes as he embraced me, saying You have Samoula's face and form, but Allimades' steadfast soul looks forth from your eyes. Welcome, my daughter."

The other members of the family received me kindly, and when I entered the dwelling entreated me to take the highest seat. After a brief hour, in which our hearts were comforted by words of counsel and affection, I arose to take leave, but the Prophet detained me, saying, "Will you not stay with us, daughter of my beloved brother? There is one vacant room in the Tebah; surely it was reserved for you."

As I endeavored to frame a reply, Japheth came quickly to my side, and added his eloquent entreaties to those of his father. His eyes beamed with anxious love, his glowing face reflected the blush which was on my cheeks. "The vacant room, dear cousin, adjoins my own; let it be yours. My brothers have chosen companions, but I am still alone. Without your sweet presence, so shall I ever remain, for none but Aloma can become the bride of Japheth."

Taking courage, I replied: "By the ties of family and affection, by the bonds of worship and sympathy, by the presence of impending danger, I am yours; but for the moment our paths diverge. I must return to my mother. I shall come to you again, if God wills it to be so." Japheth would have accompanied me. "The way is full of peril" he said. But I declined, answering, "Fear not, my guard is strong."

Then bidding my friends farewell, I hastened along the streets, which now showed signs of awakening life, and soon reached the Palace. As I entered the chamber, to my surprise I found Uronion, the husband of Minerva, awaiting my return, in whose countenance I noted a grave shadow. His features were overcast with melancholy. He presented me a linen scroll sent by Minerva, which I opened, and in astonishment read as follows:

"Peace be with you, Aloma, child of Heaven. Your coming was the dawn of light to one long overshadowed with that gloom which is the penalty of sin. The dew of your pure youth fell upon my parched and blackened heart. The light of your innocent smile warmed to life the withered blossoms of love and pity; but far better than all, your simple piety awoke the faith of my childhood. With horror I reviewed my life, and repented.

"Minerva, inmate of the Palace of Light, sought the Prophet of God, received his exhortation, and accepted his faith. I well knew the penalty—death, swift and dreadful; the fatal summons was not delayed. This moment Eldero and his band stand at my chamber door, the subterranean cave awaits me. You will see me no more.

"I send by Uronion (who still has some love and pity), in token of my grateful love, a chest I have long preserved, the only reminiscence of my early life, a present from my royal father. Keep it, dear Aloma, and sometimes think of Minerva, but never with grief. If I die at the hands of demons by God's will, all is well. I have hope in His mercy that I shall yet live again. Farewell!"

Tears blinded my eyes as I received from the hands of Uronion a chest containing various utensils necessary for woman's handiwork. "He said sadly, "I could not save Minerva. Today I leave this accursed place and return to the kingdom of Zaradis. Hesperus is next to Satanas in power. He can protect Aloma." "O Uronion" I entreated, "can you not believe in the God of Minerva?" "No," he answered gloomily, and departed.

I was now distracted by grief and regret, for there came into my mind the visit in the eastern tower, when I saw the wretched victims driven by the priests of Satanas to the death-sacrifice, and held that discourse with Minerva which led to her disobedience of the laws of the Palace. Was I not in some measure to blame? She must be rescued—but in what manner could I give her aid? Uronion is helpless, Satanas unrelenting; to appear in his presence would increase his displeasure. Hesperus is powerful, but from him I could ask no favor. Must Minerva be abandoned to her fate? The idea was intolerable.

Afterward I became more calm, and reflected that in the confusion produced by the entrance of the princes with their trains, the attention of every one, even the cruel Priests of Satanas, would be absorbed and the sacrifice forgotten. Then could Uronion, who was familiar with every passage through the subterranean vaults, make his way to Minerva and undiscovered carry her to a place of safety. But where was Uronion, the Deva? He had left me in despair, determined to quickly leave Balonia. There must be no moment of delay.

I rushed into the halls and to my agitated inquiries received answer that he had gone to the eastern tower. I hastened, to Minervas apartment but he was not there. I ran through the galleries to the court, and when near the gate, a man informed me that he had met Uronion on his way to the Tower of Satanas, where Lord Hesperus transacted the business of state.

All who could move had flocked to the city to witness the entrance of the royal trains, and unobserved I flew along the deserted street, climbed the rock, and almost breathless reached the Tower. The gate was opened. I entered, and quickly ascended the long stairway leading to the chambers. Here I found a door, and opening it cautiously, for a moment forgot my errand through astonishment and wonder. I stood beneath a vast representation of the heavens; the dome was of azure, deep as midnight, and upon it were suspended gold and silver orbs, like the sun, moon and stars. The walls were hung with gorgeous drapery, against which were placed weapons of war and instruments of unknown service.

At the farther extremity of this vaulted chamber was a throne, and ranged upon the sides were raised floors after the manner of halls of council. Doors also opened within. I barely had time to make a quick survey when voices issuing from another chamber recalled my wandering sense and filled me with alarm. I could not be mistaken; Hesperus and Uronion were in the next apartment engaged in earnest conversation. Frightened at the recklessness which had led me to such a place and full of apprehension if I were discovered, I shrank behind a large pillar, and was entirely screened from sight. Presently a door opened and the speakers came forth.

"The Preacher is guarded by the Almighty, we can not molest him," said Hesperus gravely; "but vengeance must overtake the daring one who leaves the Palace of Light to listen to his fables. The offense of Minerva is unpardonable."

"But, my lord" said Uronion (I trembled at his words), "Minerva did not go alone alone. The Princess Aloma was her companion. Together they drove through the streets of the city, and coming out on the farther side, impelled by curiosity, or perhaps by the desire of the young girl, they stopped to listen. O my lord, you know not the passion of love, and fail to appreciate my distress

"The daughter of the queen accompanied Minerva?" said Hesperus with heightened interest.

Then, musing, he continued, "Perchance love in my heart has awakened pity. O Uronion, I am not insensible to your distress. Take this key to the outer entrance to the vaults; go while the guards are gazing at the procession. Liberate Minerva, and fly with all speed. Listen!—the trumpets announcing the Devas as they approach the city. Satanas holds today a grand consultation; marriage pageants are of little consequence in light of the danger which now threatens."

The object of my coming was accomplished, but when I would have fled, a misty wall uprose on every side, and in its shade my form vanished from sight. By this token I knew I was safe, and repeating mentally the words, "Over the righteous soul the Devas have no power," I leaned against the pillar and remained motionless.

Council of the Devas

The descending footsteps of Uronion had barely faded away when the tramp of armed Darvands, the bright flashes of fire and the musical voices of the Devas announced the presence of Satanas and his associates. They came, a band of celestial forms, clad in angelic livery, princely and resplendent, with words and voices of heavenly sweetness. Their eyes flashed unearthly fire; their airy footsteps gave no echo. Upon each royal brow blazed its own peculiar star, set with the color of its nativity; but in the features could be seen lines traced by centuries of unrestrained passion and despotic power. Princes of the East and of the West, of the North and of the South, Kings, Guardians, and others of unknown names.

But where is the Monarch of the Waters? No answer; but from afar a sound as of the booming of the sea in a rising storm. The warrior sons retired, and the proud Devas bowed before the throne. And now a change—each form looms indistinct, each voice grows terrible. I had come to this place to speak to Uronion; I must witness a council of Devas. I hear with every nerve strained. I tremble and falter but the friendly column supports me. Remember, repeat, if you can, Aloma! Listen! Listen! it's the voice of Satanas.

In some distant, awful hour he dared to strive against the Creator and aspire to His Almighty glory. Who but the Light-bearer would presume to soar so high? Swelling with pride, he revolted and attracted to his banner myriads of the host of Heaven. They subjugated the human race, under his instruction, won the love of women, and established a sovereignty. For many centuries their kingdom has remained undisturbed, but now the enemy is roused, and gloomy danger threatens.

He calls upon Agnaris, the god of Fire. Swift, subtle, uncertain, he moves forward, his step marked by a scorched footprint. On his head gleams no star, but in place thereof a crown of thin flames. His eyeballs glow like living coals, his voice is hollow and gusty. The Devas shrink from his hot breath, all but the lord Satanas, before whose piercing glance Agnaris grows pale and almost disappears. He bids the great Master look to the stars that draw upon their central fires, which struggle to be free. They heave the bed of ocean; they strive to burst the ribs of earth; the demons cannot restrain their fury.

Agnaris disappears, vanishes in space, and the aerial voice of Prince Owadu is heard. In his realm is a great planet uninhabited, cracked and fissured, deep—seamed and rent by volcanic fire. Deep, jarring, splitting sounds now issue from the center of this desolate planet; it is about to fall to pieces. Its disruption will endanger the earth.

Hesperus is called. He, ranging in the twilight hour along the bounds of day and darkness, beholds with alarm a strange mustering of the Heavenly host, The balance of the worlds is unsettled, the Earth is threatened with dire catastrophe. Tempests will prevail; a great deluge will come, by the breaking of the last great watery canopy which envelops the Earth, letting in a mighty flood of waters.

A cry of horror burst from all the band, succeeded by a hush of fear. Then like waves that growl above the wreck, spoke Zorabah, darkest and most fierce Deva. He would abandon this troublesome world, leave it to the wrath of Jehovah; he scorned men, and detested women and children. In his realm, he said, is an unpopulated world of exceeding beauty. There, free from the Lord of Heaven, he would establish a kingdom greater and more glorious.

But Satanas in wrath rebuked the other. He will yield nothing to the Lord of Heaven; not even shall the approaching marriage be deferred. Nothing but utter ruin can change his purpose. He owns the Earth; he holds it by might. If it be destroyed in the fury of the elements, so be it. He defies the Eternal to destroy what he alone controls!

Ah, how are you so blinded and deceived, O fallen Spirit, once so wise!

And now Satanas rouses the courage of the other Devas by recounting the triumphs of former struggles, their passion by mention of their beautiful wives and children, their pride by thought of province and power. They must convert the Eternal's expected victory into failure, and thus extend their rank to the splendors of the highest heaven.

The Strong One is bound by His own law, was the argument; by that Law they must precipitate the hour of doom! Then follow words vague and awful, like rushing meteors and roaring winds, not to be written, not to be recalled, whose import I could barely comprehend. I only knew that by a desperate plot which involved the destruction of other planets, Earth's calamity might be averted.

Satanas ceased, and heavy thunder shook the dome; fire and smoke filled the vault; but, rising above the turmoil, I heard this dreadful blasphemy:

"Honor to our Light-bearer!
Praise to the Way—Preparer!
Glory to the God—Darer!
Satanas, our King!"

Again was heard the voice of the great Prince—"Who will lead?" All cried, "Hesperus! Hesperus!" Hesperus answered: "And hereafter reign, the equal of Satanas the King." The fires burned low, and the features of the great King grew dark, but he answered grandly: "Agreed, right royal prince. You only, besides Satanas, can discern the forces. You, Hesperus, never clouded by fumes or Homa, never shaken with throbs of passion!

"Summon my associates in peril and glory; seven is the mystic number. Command Loeda and Orba, fear not to call Koradin the mighty. At midnight depart; you who do not care for banqueting. Away! Away! Our peril admits no delay."

Amid flashing lights and sounds that jarred the Tower, with words and signs obscure and awful, the Devas departed, all but the Lord Hesperus, who retired to his chamber and closed the door.

This was my moment for flight, but by reason of fear and astonishment I was rendered powerless. However, the reflection that delay would but increase the danger of discovery gave me supernatural strength. Noiselessly I crept from my place of concealment and safely outside the gate of the Tower, flew rather than ran to my retreat in the Palace. Once only I dared to glance backward. I had not been discovered. Upon the dizzy height of the dome stood Hesperus alone. His eyes, which appeared white, earnestly scanned the vault of heaven. Absorbed, motionless, he strove to forecast the possibilities of the tomorrow.

Hesperus and Satanas

Evening had now fallen upon the earth. The day, sultry and hot, was over, and exhausted by its extraordinary adventures, I threw off the upper wrap with which, since coming to Balonia, I had always concealed my head and bosom, removed the vest, and loosening my hair, enabling it to flow to my feet. How like it is to Samoula's! I untied my sandals, and for a few moments enjoyed the rest and freedom of solitude. The Palace of Light overlooked the city, and as my chamber was in the highest tower, no intruding eye could violate its seclusion, though the latticed door where I sat was opened wide upon the small balcony to admit the evening air.

"For the moment," I exclaimed, "I am alone and safe, but oh, what danger and wrath hang over the world! I hear advancing footsteps. The Avenger hastens, the day of woe is at hand. How great is our exposure and peril! O my mother, we sleep upon a volcano; we are curtained by stormclouds; pitfalls and snares are beneath our feet! How shall we escape destruction? O my God, how shall we escape?"

Then, retiring to the shadow of the chamber, I knelt to pray—"O God of Allimades, lead me unstained from this city of Sin! Show me a way of escape, even if it be by the dreary gate of Death! But not for myself alone would I implore your mercy. My mother—though she die, save her from further sin! O You Most Holy, restore her to righteousness, undefiled by the embrace of Satanas! And for one other would I dare to lift up my voice. O God of infinite mercy, Hesperus whom you created for glory. His sin is not so dreadful as that of his associates in rebellion. O compassionate One, give him power to repent, restore him to your love, make him again a bright angel, strong to do your service, loving you more than others of the Heavenly host, who will not know the joy of pardoned sin!"

At this instant I became conscious of a presence in the room, and heard a breathing like a deep-drawn sigh. Hastily arising, I saw in the doorway of the balcony, distinctly revealed against the evening sky, the form of Hesperus. There was a rustle, a slight upward motion, and the form vanished. My heart beat thick with alarm, and my cheeks grew hot with shame. Hesperus, wishing to say farewell before his perilous undertaking, had come to the tower. He had seen me disrobed, had heard my prayer! The sigh—was it from wounded love or penitent sorrow?

Far too anxious and agitated for sleep, I wrapped myself in a mantle and went out upon the balcony. Presently I heard voices below in earnest conversation. I could not see the speakers, but I recognized the now familiar voice of Hesperus. "I can serve you no longer; though this decision is made at a moment when peril stimulates courage, you cannot accuse me of cowardice!"

"Can a Deva know madness?" asked Satanas, in a tone of incredulity. "I but return to sanity and duty," answered the other. "The Almighty Law is eternal it cannot be broken. We are not revolutionists, but rebels, who conspire against a beneficent Ruler. I repent; I shall resist no more."'

"And this to one who exalts you above all others, who now makes you his equal? Have you asked favor of the Eternal—you who have ravished the earth, defied His law, blasphemed His name—you, the Counselor of Satanas?"

"I do not know," returned Hesperus. "I remember that I have sinned; I shall sin no more." "Prince of the West," exclaimed Satanas, "this change is but the weakness of newborn passion. Aloma affects piety for her own purpose. She is but human, as you may soon see. "Lord Satanas," said Hesperus with dignity, "the love of woman may sink an Angel to ruin, or bear him upward to the gates of glory."

"The damsel has bewitched you. Accursed the hour in which she did not perish with her father. She shall die when Samoula is wholly mine!" exclaimed his lord.

"Until the rites are celebrated I remain in your service, though Zaradis, as he desires, shall command the Mystic Seven. You, know now, O Satanas, Aloma, like the Prophet, is secure, guarded by the power of the Omnipotent One."

The Pageant

Coronation morning rose. At break of day the great court was astir with workmen and Darvands who were to complete the preparations. As my windows opened upon this court, the noise awakened me, and I rose and watched their labor. Towers, walls, houses and hanging gardens, all bore a festive appearance. Flags and ensigns fluttered in the breeze, garlands hung from the shaft of the great serpent, flowering shrubs and vines filled every projection, and the air was heavy with perfume. Across the great arches were the banners, with tinkling bells wrought into the significant words:

"Satanas and Samoula"
"Queen of the Earth."
"Bride of the Sun."

Gilded pavilions were made ready to receive the queens of the other Devas, and in the center of the court rose a great throne, upon which Satanas was to crown Samoula his Bride and Queen. This throne, of more than human grandeur, rested upon the backs of four brazen dragons, from whose mouths flowed a perpetual stream of Homa. There were no steps to the throne, but from a wide opening in the wall of the Palace, leading directly to it, was an aerial pathway resembling a broad sunbeam.

As I observed these wonders, a sudden hush pervaded the court. Each workman suspended his labor, and a subdued murmur ran through the crowd: "Make way, make way! Ormandu, the Prince of the Winds, comes!" The place was vacant in a moment, and an awful form, indistinct and shapeless, descended from the air to complete the decorations. Closely screened by the lattice, I fled not, but breathlessly observed his motions, wondering there with great amazement. He beckoned the clouds; they came, and he shook out their folds; he called the winds, and they rushed to obey his mandates; in the vast cavern of his mouth were they confined until driven forth to do his bidding. Across his vague shoulders were flung iris—hued bows, and his quiver held forked lightnings.

With tremendous force he began to work, raising from the corner towers tall columns of vapors, white and glistening as the foam of the ocean. These he united by prismatic arches thrown across the court, meeting at a point above the throne. Over the lofty dome thus formed, this awful being stretched a cloud—curtain rosy in hue, which softened while it did not obscure the light. From the bosom of this cloud were reflected a thousand opaline tints, dissolving, blending, as the mass swayed in the breeze.

An occasional flash of light or a dash of hail gave intimation of danger, and explained the terror this Presence inspired. He vanished like a shadow, and a long time I remained entranced by the changeful aspects of his wonderful creation, unmindful of the passing hours, and unobservant of the assembly now thronging the court, pavilion, roof and terrace.

The spell was sharply broken by a messenger, who came in a hurry to inform me that my presence was required by the queen. Thereupon I obeyed the summons, and was taken through a screened garden into an inner chamber exceeding all others in splendor and magnificence.

Over the alabaster walls and vaulted ceiling ran a golden trellis covered with mimic vines and flowers painted in divers colors, perfumed with mist and sprinkled with gems like star-dust.

Beneath a canopy of silver face, the couch of down was spread; around the apartment were placed gold and ivory furniture, mirrors and statues, and above all, curtains of azure, adjusted for shade or seclusion.

Within this atmosphere of light and shadow, color and perfume, stood the royal pair, unapproachable in majesty and beauty. The world had never seen a vision of such transcendent glory. Satanas, the Light-bearer, was attired in a robe of heavenly blue, bedecked with diamonds and jeweled fringe that swept the floor like dancing flames. Upon his forehead blazed a pentacle of starry gems, from which issued a spray as it were a fountain of fire, and in his hand was held a sceptre set with similar glory, while from every jewel-point quivered and flashed the light peculiar to his majestic presence.

Samoula, as Dawn, recipient and reflector of light, was draped, or, rather, enshrouded, in garments rosy and nebulous as the cloud now overhanging the Palace. In every blushing fold lay pearls, white and lustrous, and a veil of mist and sparkling light, secured upon her forehead by a coronet of sapphire, covered but did not conceal the golden hair which rippled to her feet. Her eyes were large and brilliant like stars, her color tinted like the flush of day, and when she moved, a perfume floated in the air, sweet as the breath of morning. Beautiful Samoula, incarnation of woman's grace and loveliness, my tears fall fast for you!

While Hesperus, grave and silent, received the orders of Satanas, I conversed with my mother apart.

"Aloma," she began, in gentle chiding tones, "why are you still in rustic garb, ill-suited to this festal day? Array yourself quickly in robes of state, that your presence and beauty may grace our coronation." I kissed her hand in humility, and answered, "O my mother, assuredly God has given me power to pierce the veil of the future; to perceive that which cannot be apprehended by outward sense. By this I am warned to take no part in these scenes. Forgive me as I observe you at a distance; my heart is with you even to the end."

"My child", she said, " your words fill me with alarm! They are the clear echo of a dull voice within me, a reproof, a menace; my conscience is troubled, my reason is clouded. I am driven forward by an irresistible power, tangled in a net from which I cannot extricate myself. I fear Satanas my haughty lord, yet I must obey his will. O that Allimades still lived!" At this, the only allusion to my father she had ever made, we were both greatly agitated. I restrained myself with difficulty, and soothed her, saying—"The evil is irreparable: the diet of the Palace, its baths and perfumes, I have taken none of them, and can perceive clearly that the future will execute the decrees of the Most High. Let us hold fast the thread of faith Allimades placed in our hands, and it will lead us, let us hope, even through fire and blood, safe to the haven of eternal rest, in God's good time." "Pray for me, my daughter," she answered, greatly moved. "I have lost the power of prayer. We must part, I fear, forever. Farewell! Farewell!"

At this moment the shaft of the revolving serpent made no shadow; it was the high noon. The sounding trumpets announced that all was in readiness. Satanas took the hand of Samoula. Together they floated through the long corridor, through the broad doorway, down the aerial pavement, to their place upon the golden throne.

Profound silence reigned throughout the vast assemblage as Satanas removed from his sceptre the diamond spray, placed it in the coronet which encircled the brow of Samoula, saying, "Thus do I create you my companion, the perfection of beauty, Bride of Satanas, Queen of the Earth and Sun."

At that instant the cloud—screen overhead was cut in two, and a blaze of light streamed upon the royal pair, conferring such dazzling brilliance that the astonished multitude, after a moment of stupefaction, burst into a storm of applause, shouting, "A god! a goddess!

Glory to Samoula, peerless in beauty! Glory to Satanas, Light—creator, King of the Earth and the Sun!"

This blasphemous adulation of created beings filled me with horror, a feeling which seemed to find voice in a growl of thunder from a black cloud overhead, as it suddenly closed together.

And now the blare of trumpets announced the approach of the tribute—bearers, an almost interminable procession, who were this day to lay the treasures of earth and sea at the feet of the mighty Prince. The giant sons of Satanas led the van, their athletic forms clad in silver scales, and on their heads nodding plumes. Fair were they in complexion, with light, curling locks; for though the numerous wives of Satanas had been of every style of beauty, the sons resembled their royal fathers. They were mounted upon horses, whose black, glossy bodies were thickly dappled with spots, and whose fierce, rolling eyes and airy thread seemed to scorn the earth.

Following the children of Satanas came a thousand white elephants, bearing magnificent presents to the mighty monarch. Next in rank were the sons of Owadu, in armor of burnished green, seated in superb chariots drawn by harnessed lions, whose savage nature tamely yielded to the superhuman strength and fear—inspiring voices of the terrible beings who held the reins. After them, the sons of Zaradis, Saranzis, Ramudas, and other celestial princes, all mighty men, men of renown, arrayed in the costumes of their fathers' kingdoms, presenting magnificent offerings to the King of earthly princes.

Snatches of conversation were wafted to my ears from various men and women in the vast assemblage, comments upon the debaucheries of the Devas, and the Darvands, their brutal and wicked sons. The words showed me all too plainly the corruption of mind created in the speakers. Shame and indignation filled my soul as I drew my veil close and shrank back, realizing more fully than ever the appalling condition of the world under this perverted angelic sway. Truly these beings made the earth tremble; they shake the kingdoms, and destroy the government thereof; they listen not to the cry of the prisoner! Dazzled by the magnificence of the Devas and their giant offspring, overawed by their unscrupulous tyranny, men have abandoned the struggle, and drift with the stream of ungodliness. They say: "The Lord has forgotten the earth, the Lord does not see."

Yet the Prophet has ceased not to warn them that the day of wrath approaches; and now the fatal decree has gone forth. Even at this moment of exultation the footsteps of the Avenger echo along the pathway of time.

Through the long afternoon, amid applause of the gazing throng, the brilliant procession streamed past, bearing the wealth and glory of the world. Chariots and horses, camels and cattle, rare and curious animals from every clime, bundles of fur, bales of richest fabrics, broidered vestments, mirrors, vases, chests of gems, gold and silver, coral, amber and treasures of the sea, baskets of fruits, strange plants, spices, perfumes, and a band of dancers and beautiful captives.

And now appeared a culminating wonder—a fleet of air-ships, winging their flight above the great assembly! These marvelous structures are the invention of a mighty Darvand who discovered in the hollow bones of birds that which would have escaped the eyes of mere mortals, the secret of flight. It has been carefully concealed, and the use of these aerial barges confined to the royal families with whose colors they are superbly decorated.

Upon the bow of each barge stood a beautiful queen, who, as the ships paused on fluttering sails before the throne, gracefully dropped at the feet of the newly crowned empress tokens of admiration and loyalty. As the fleet slowly sailed away and disappeared in the overhanging mist, a strain of angelic music from the Devas proclaimed the triumph of rebellion and sensuality. O sin and shame, the dreadful guilt lauded by angel tongues!

The pageant was ended, the feast was to begin. The sun, which, through its canopy of mist, had all day long looked calmly down upon this scene of splendor, now sank in the west. Above the descending spheres tolled upward billowy clouds of crimson hue; the ruddy glow stained tower and pavilion, marble colonnade and house-top. And thus, when Satanas and his bride passed up the luminous pathway into the banquet hall, Samoula appeared immersed in a crimson tide. "Too red, too red!" abruptly exclaimed Aldeth. "My mistress seems bathed in blood!"

RETRIBUTION

The sun went down, the crimson faded and deepened to purple, gray shadows fell, and with a shiver I retired to the solitude of my own chamber, while Aldeth prepared a simple meal. Before it was finished the confusion and uproar in the banquet—hall became so great that I trembled for the safety of my mother. 'Go, Aldeth," I cried, "linger near Samoula. You may be of service to your mistress, and I shall be less anxious." Left alone, I went forth upon the balcony and gave myself up to melancholy reflections.

Could I do nothing for my mother? She was now irrevocably bound to Satanas. In the All-Powerful God alone was help. I looked out upon the heavens. Twilight had faded into night. As my heart went out to God in prayer, a passing thrill gave token that the fetters of sense were removed. I saw celestial forms soaring upward, radiant and pure, though powerful as those of the Devas. A tremor fills the air; it wavers, faints, and dies—again it swells upon the breeze. Is it rising wind, moaning among the palms? No! No! Celestial voices float earthward from the vanishing cloud—words are formed; they weave a requiem—the warp is music, the woof a sigh.

Song of the Angels

Mourn—for the Star of Day

Dieth at dawn;
Weep—for the Moon's soft ray
Paleth ere morn.
No rosy blush may rise,
No perfume-breathed sighs;
The burning kiss,
The dream of bliss
To anguish turn.

Behold—the mists of death

Now darken heaven;
Listen—the roaring waves
Are madly driven!
And shrieks of wild despair
Convulse the shivering air;
Life's flame expires;
The natal fires

No longer burn!
The giant sons must die;
The Lords of Light
In caverns dark must lie,
In rayless night.
E'en Mercy sighs, "Too late!"
'Neath prison bars they wait,
In blind dismay,
The dreadful day
That seals their fate!

Like the last quiver of a bell the sound dies in the distance. But who is he that remains enwrapped in mournful thought? His face is stern and sad, his hand rests upon the handle of a sword, his black garments rustle in the night-breeze like withered leaves, and his voice, blending with the melancholy sound, whispers—

"O hand, be firm; heart, be unrelenting; yes do execute the decrees of the Most High."

Who is he that joins not his peers in their flight from the doomed earth? It is Azelles, Angel of Death, Angel of the Lord!

I close my heavy eyes, and press my throbbing heart; my thoughts revert to Allimades resting beneath the cypress trees. O that I were lying unconscious by his side!

The Beginning of the End

There was but one moment to dream, for now an awful uproar arose throughout the Palace—shouts, curses, yells; then a confused crowd rushed madly into the garden, men and giants uttering unintelligible cries.

Towering above all others, the mighty celestials pressed forward, rage and fury depicted on their dreadful faces.

And look! the fountain of fire in the midst of the garden, moved by some infernal influence, shot up furiously into the sky, lighting with unnatural glare the great court, the palace and surrounding heights—a fearful mockery of day. The struggling crowd surged and howled forth oaths and blasphemies so horrible that I pressed my hands upon my ears to shut out the stunning words. In vain did I oppose such feeble barriers, for high above all other sounds was heard the voice of Satanas rallying the Devas.

"To arms, to arms, celestials! The hour of fate hastens, but we will foil our hated Foe. Yet will I ascend and be like the Most High! To my victorious allies will I give the kingdoms of the world and its glory. Aladdis, the hour has come! Loosen the Steeds of the Sun!"

The vaulted dome re-echoed the voice, terrible as a roll of thunder; shouts from the maddened Devas answered the appeal, fires flashed from heaven-forged armor, and the clash of alarms swelled the air. The winged Deva sped toward Mount Hermon and uttered a piercing cry, which was answered by a roar beneath the mountain, so furious that the Palace shook and the crowds shrieked with fear. The doors of the vault burst with a clang, and there rushed forth, like the blast of a furnace, horses of fire winged with flame. Driven by the wind, they assumed strange, distorted shapes, smoke and light issued from their nostrils as they rapidly approached the Palace.

I grew terrified and turned to flee, when a fearful sight held me motionless. On the wall of the garden stood a dark and gloomy form, whose features of deepest melancholy, seen by sudden flashes of the Fire Fountain, I recognized to be those of Hesperus. Satanas also perceived him and springing forward, he swung the sharp sword above his head. "Traitor," he shouted, "mount upwards, and receive your honor and fortune!" "Traitor no longer," returned Hesperus; "loyal at last to my rightful King."

With a howl of rage, Satanas disappeared from view. I was soon aroused by the excited entrance of our old servant, Aldeth, who began in breathless terror, "My child, awful omens have been seen. Shortly were the king and queen seated at the banquet, when a messenger (sent to inquire why the Homa fountain had ceased to flow) came in haste and informed Satanas that the water in the wells had suddenly sunk and the bed of the river was dry.

"'Strike off the head of the liar,' commanded the enraged king. 'My lord,' replied the Counselor, 'death on a wedding day is but an evil omen.' Satanas paused: not so the sword of the executioner. One swift blow, and the head of the unfortunate messenger rolled upon the floor.

"A strange light now filled the banquet-hall, and on the ceiling ran letters of fire traced by no mortal hand. The green serpent in the golden tank threw himself violently out of the water, his red crest erect, and with horrible hissing and convulsions expired.

"At this moment Zorabah a high ranking Deva rushed in. His countenance was distorted by rage, and he roared like the roar of a mighty wind. 'Drunken fools,' he cried, 'forgetful of our tremendous venture, you are wasting away moments upon which hang the fate of Eternity, I could hate you as I hate the weak race to which your sensual bodies are enslaved! Driveling idiots, leave your women and banqueting! Zaradis and his force have been forced to flee. Up and away! Unless you act at once with mighty vigor, all is lost! lost! lost!!!'

"Without waiting to reprove the presumptuous Zorabah, Satanas, with all the other Devas, sprang from the table, seized their armor, and exchanging fearful words and tokens, rushed forth. The ladies moved the queen from the hall before I could gain access to her." While Aldeth yet spoke, a piercing scream rang out through the now empty corridors, a cry, of mortal anguish. Startled from the paralyzed condition into which I had fallen, I flew along the halls, followed closely by the frighten Aldeth, the song of the Angels resounding in memory—

Weep—for the Moon's soft ray
Paleth ere morn."

We reached the door of the bridal chamber. O sight of woe! There, prone upon the marble floor, lay the beautiful form of my mother, writhing in the agonies of death. The steel sword had done its work, the lifeblood poured fast from the cruel wound in her bosom. Yet she was still conscious, and as I, sobbing, embraced her, she whispered faintly—"Saved, O my daughter!" Then her violet eyes were closed in death.

Frantic with grief and terror, I dashed away the restraining arms of Aldeth, and rushed out into the pale moonlight. All was quiet in court and palace, but far away could be heard a confused sound like the surges of ocean. As I passed the wall from which a few moments previous I had seen the form of Hesperus, I groaned aloud—"O night of death and woe! O my mother! O Hesperus! O my God!"

A deep sigh answered, and from the dense shadow of the wall came back the words: "O my God!"

There was such sorrow in the tone that, forgetting my own grief and fear, I turned toward the spot from where the sound proceeded, and there, pale but firm in courage, stood Hesperus. I hastened to his side, and for an instant he took my hand and pressed it closely in his.

"Aloma, I repent fully of my disloyalty to God. Nevermore will I be a rebel against my holy Creator. No more will I take the form of a human. I must again assume my normal spirit condition. I shall never forget you. Now I must say, Good-bye, and may God be ever with you!" In a moment Hesperus had vanished, and I stood alone.

The Prophetess Aloma's Vision

Raising my heart in thankfulness to God I quickly sped along, not knowing where I was going. The men of the city, uncertain of purpose, had fled to the Tower of Satanas, and a hushed fear, as of some impending calamity, had fallen on the women and children. I did not pause until I found myself beyond the limits of the deserted city, and coming upon an open plain, gazed long and earnestly into the southern sky. By the tremor that agitated my frame, by the increasing luminosity of the dim stars, by a clearer vision of the shrouded full moon, and by the intensified quickening of every sense, I was conscious of the superhuman power.

Then, in vision, I went out, past sun and moon, past grand and solemn planets, through fields of drifting stars, out into cold and darksome space, until I hung upon the verge of God's eternity. I perceived the Invisible, the Inaudible, the Intangible, that which unaided mortal sense can never comprehend.

I looked upon the Energies of Nature! Wheels within wheels, forever turning, changing, returning. Impalpable resistance, imponderable weight. Nor night nor discord, age or death. Swift as thought, firm as the will of God. There dwells Eternal Order! There dwells Eternal Noon!

Beneath a dome clear as crystal I saw the Dial of Time. Here is where the centuries are measured, here are recorded the immeasurable eternities. And above all was the Great Center of the Universe which binds the sweet influences of the celestial bodies. At this sight I trembled and cried out with fear. But a mighty angel answered my fear, saying, "Only God alone can loosen the bands established by his Eternal Will. Child of earth, look westward."

Straining my eyes through the limitless heavens, I perceived a long line of worlds, stretching in almost endless continuity. One immense star was wheeling into place, silent, sublime, awful!

In a moment more the angel spoke again. "Behold, O child of earth!" I followed with my eyes to where he directed with his golden wand. His eyes were fastened on the great Dial, and following their inclination, I perceived that the mark was slowly sinking to the lowest point of the great circle, beneath which in letters black as night, I discerned the inscription—"The Hour of Doom"

Again I followed the solemn eyes of the angel, which now were fixed with intense eagerness upon a luminous spot high above the atmosphere of the earth. There, like a phantom host in battle array, I saw the rebel angels upon their steeds of flame, and by his superior brightness knew that Satanas held command. In the thickest of the conflict between the powers of darkness and the powers of light, the towering form of the great opponent of God flashed forth a blaze that dazzled and appalled all who opposed him. O intense demoniacal rage, O majestic wrath of Heaven, how can any mortal speak of their power!

Before this infernal blast of demon-fury the angelic band seemed to slowly give way, and the triumphant voice of Satanas, clear but distant, rang out like a mighty trumpet.

"Princes of Satanas, the battle is won; the earth is ours! We defy the Strong One! We will yet reign in power equal to the Eternal upon His Throne!"

Then the heavens and the earth was shaken, the stars grew pale and circled more slowly on their wheels of fire! All nature shuddered at the possible consummation. At this moment a sudden hush, a pulseless silence, fell on all created things, as from the northern sky, stretching across the transparent heavens, there appeared—the Shadow of a Hand!

Without delay or haste, the Shadow moved forward and fell upon the host of demons, who, elated with their assurance of victory, perceived not its advance. Suddenly a spasm as of cold passed over them, the fire slowly faded, ashy pallor overspread every face, their strong pinions drooped, as their weapons fell from their nerveless hands, despair took possession of each of these fallen angels.

Colder and darker grew the host, sinking lower and lower, when, with the suddenness of a flash of light, a great comet, which in the absorbing interest of this supreme moment had been rapidly approaching unseen, swerved to one side and gradually circled around them, condensing and hardening as it passed under the Shadow of the Hand, until they were hopelessly encompassed and bound.

A faint blue flame parting from the one time Light-bearer gave token of the last struggle, as deeper and darker the incarnation of despair sank into the rayless gloom of the black, unfathomable abyss of earth's atmosphere.

The Shadow then moved until it reached the crystal dome; and then the pointer on, the dial trembled to the Hour of Doom. Too late, too late, to save the kingdom of the Devas! All is lost! Again deep silence fell on all created things; then, like the solemn chime of bells came voices of the Heavenly hosts in harmonious chant: "Glory, glory, forevermore! You alone are mighty, Lord God creator of all things!"

When I awoke I was as one dead, without sense or motion, lying prone upon the cold earth.

* * * *

How long I was insensible I do not know but with returning consciousness I heard the voices of men in great agitation. "It surely seems:' said one, "that the old prophets words are coming true. What does it all mean?" "Lets go quickly! Where shall we go? Where is Satanas? In terror they ran forward, stumbling in the darkness, very much afraid

At this moment of perplexity as I stood in bewilderment, not knowing where to turn, I heard one calling my name—"Aloma, Aloma!" Sweeter than the music of an angel was the voice coming through the gloomy night.

"O Japheth," I cried, as I fell into his extended arms, "my mother is murdered, the north tower is burned, Aldeth must have perished!"

"But I am with you, my beloved," said he; "the barriers that separated us are removed, will you be mine?" And I answered, "Dear Japheth, I am yours."

Carefully we groped our way along toward the Tebah into which Japheth told me the family were now heading. He also informed me that being near the Palace when the alarm was sounded, he entered the halls and sought me in vain; but among the women who had gathered around the body of the murdered queen was poor Aldeth, almost stupefied with terror.

He roused her and together they went to my chamber, hoping that I might have fled. Not finding me, Japheth proposed that all my belongings should be removed from the Palace to the habitation of the Prophet, to which it was possible I might have retreated. Being convinced that the great catastrophe was near, he hired some idlers who stood in the halls, and soon everything was transferred to the Tebah. But I was not there; whereupon old Aldeth went back to await my return. Sadly, it was to meet her fate, for in a few minutes the tower fell and all within perished. What caused its fall is not known. Faithful old servant and friend! She has gone to her rest.

Meantime Japheth sought me through the darkness, directed by a peculiar glow which encircled my head. The nature of this he did not understand, but in my heart I felt that it was the lingering glory of the vision given me. Trembling and weary, we reached the much-desired haven, where our anxious friends gave us a gracious welcome. None questioned as to my absence from the Palace and I told the vision to none; to no other human eye was it revealed. After some much needed refreshment, I retired to the little room Japheth had unwittingly prepared for my reception. Here, among the articles so hastily removed from my chamber in the Palace, I found my journal and before the events of this day of wonders fade from my memory, I confide to it the secrets I can entrust to no other.

This night, by the solemn words of the Prophet and my own irrevocable vow, I have been united to Japheth in the sacred bonds of marriage. The unusual circumstances hastened this event. An unparalleled tragedy is about to transpire. The desolation of a world!

Was there ever a wedding done under such ominous conditions? Was ever a marriage journey so begun? Our love had birth in danger and gloom, dire portents in earth and heaven attend our nuptials, and shrouded horror hangs over the race of men. May that powerful Hand, whose shadow can sink to despair the hosts of mighty Satanas, control the elements now gathering for devastation and carry us safely through that perilous voyage in which there is neither map nor chart, rudder nor compass, sun nor star, to guide.

The memory of this night's experience overpowers me; I can hardly trust my own recollection. Was it an illusion, or have I indeed been permitted to behold the Spirit World and witness the mystery and majesty of

God's Power in the energies of Nature? As I look forth into the night and upward to Him, the answer and assurance is given. Slowly, fearfully, I turn to the West. There, high above the dusty mountain, like a smile shining through tears, still twinkles the Evening Star!

Tebah and its Inmates

Sixth Day.

The first day of my new life is made memorable by other marvels.

We were awakened at dawn by a deep roar, as of a wild beast coming down the valley. Hurrying to the door an extraordinary sight met our eyes. A large lion with his mate stood unsure upon the bank of the river. He bent his shaggy head to the earth, smelling the ground as if he perceived something unusual, then stopped abruptly, looked up to the sky, sniffed the air, roared again and ran forward. Frightened by his savage mien, we all hastily retreated, except the Prophet, who went out to meet him.

The ferocious beast crouched low, dragged himself upon the ground and crept close to the master, fawning and rubbing against his side. The Prophet fondled the lion as he would a dog and led him unresistingly through the door of the Tebah, into a narrow stall at the farthest end of the boat. His mate passively followed; the bar was raised and they were made secure.

This event was so significant that a solemn silence fell upon us; but we had little time to consider before a loud bellow was heard and a huge elephant with his mate came plunging across the plain, throwing his trunk in the air and sniffing in fear as the lion had done. He also came near and offered himself to be led quietly to his quarters in the boat. Soon a frightened stag and doe peeped timidly over the hill and surveying our party for a moment, came to the place where we were standing; two beautiful dogs followed them, but looked not upon us, only upward at the sky and howled.

And now the valley seemed alive with animals, flocking over the hills and swarming from the groves. None molested another; all seemed urged forward by the instinct that danger was abroad and safety was with the Prophet.

The sons of Noah diligently aided the father, and without confusion the patient brutes were placed in the stalls assigned them. Presently the familiar note of a woodthrush caught my ear, and looking upward, I perceived a tree near by filled with singing birds of many species. With the enticement of grain scattered upon the ground they followed us and were easily settled in their new home.

Meantime a crowd of idlers had gathered to witness this extraordinary scene. Some, jeering the Prophet, inquired why he had concealed his magic under the pretense of piety and defied him to frighten them by this exhibition of black art. Some endeavored to drive back the animals, but were repulsed by angry growls, or a snap of the teeth too fierce to be again invited. Some looked on stupefied, while the more thoughtful seemed puzzled, and said, "Why are these wild animals behaving like this? They sniff the air as if in fear and quietly submit themselves to be imprisoned in this strange building which appears prophetically arranged for their reception. Is it possible the mad Prophet has told the truth?"

"You speak foolishly," said another. "Wonders will never cease while the world stands; these animals are governed by some law with which we are unacquainted; our wise men must be consulted."

"Let us not forestall trouble," said still another. "Believe in danger when it appears. The end comes soon enough. Notice how hot the day grows!"

Indeed, the heat had become intense, and after the hold of the vessel was full, we ceased from receiving the animals and sought refreshment and rest.

Toward evening Japheth took me to examine this marvelous building. The beasts, dull and sleepy, gave little heed to our coming, though sometimes our presence startled them giving way to a cry of fear. Their quarters are divided from those of the family by a thick wall that excludes all sound and yet is arranged to admit a sufficiency of fresh air. Food and drink are in abundant store: but, being closely confined and quiet, it is thought they will require little care.

Over fifty years was the Tebah in building, according to instructions given our venerable father Noah in a vision, which instructions were most faithfully carried out. Nothing that could contribute to our comfort has been overlooked. Many men were employed in its construction to whom it was an inexplicable mystery. The building of such an elaborate vessel was considered the height of folly by interested but unbelieving neighbors. People from hundreds of miles around would make yearly trips to see how the work was progressing and report back home on the progress, nevertheless, the Lord blessed Noah and the work prospered.

The three sons labored tirelessly to complete the Tebah at the appointed time. This exercise assisted in their developing into strong and graceful men. Many difficulties arose taxing their ingenuity. The overcoming of these increased their love and reverence for the Great Architect, whose plans they were endeavoring to carry out.

In finishing the individual apartments for the members of the family the preferences of each were lovingly considered and great was our joy at the completion of the work. My own room, though small, is beautiful. Had I expressed my preferences I could not have been so greatly pleased. The colors are soft and harmonious, the furniture simple and appropriate.

My writing materials have been placed on a beautiful little ivory table. What a wonderful little gold, diamond pointed pen! From Japheth, I suppose. Through the window with its translucent material streams the light, and it can be adjusted to admit the air. There are several ferns tastefully distributed around the room which I shall enjoy caring for, and noting their growth. My heart is full of love and joy at this moment as my husband enters and, we spend much time in loving conversation.

We have been in the Tebah for seven days and there has been a solemn hush over everything! A tense feeling of expectancy. The door is closed. This was done by an unseen hand and we know the time has arrived! How quiet everything is! The calm before the storm.

I hear voices of men and Darvands under our window. They say that wild animals are now wandering about and ravaging the country. The speakers crouch under the shadow of the Tebah, greatly terrified. Their words are frightful—they curse the heated air, they curse the Devas for their continued absence; they curse themselves, and God.

After the morning breakfast and a sacrifice of unusual solemnity, we sat for a long time in silent meditation. Soon the voice of the Prophet broke the stillness: "The time has come. Soon will the valley of Balonia and the realms of all the Devas be destroyed but we by God's mercy shall ride in safety. Thus will the Lord vindicate our faith in the eyes of all. God's wisdom will be made manifest. The multitudes have been warned in vain; they have lost their opportunity; they must die. However, there is hope for them in the future. God has revealed to me that He has a blessing for all in the distant future, providing, of course, they will at that time prove themselves worthy of the blessing. But the Darvands—their very existence is contrary to the will and law of the Lord. They must perish forever in their incorrigible wickedness. The earth will never see them more!" He paused a moment: Listen! the muttering rumble of the heavens. Even now the tempest gathers, which shall add to the horrors of the sea."

Again we became quiet as we listen to the loud complaints of the passers-by and by the noise of the animals, who instinctively, feel the coming woe. Some time ago I wrote in this journal my father's words: "Shut out of the world in this lonely forest, your life will be eventless." How rapid has been the march of events! But I cannot stop to review the past. It seems a wonderful providence of the Holy One that though I lost my parents I am surrounded by a family fast becoming as dear to me as my own. My brothers and their wives I love; at first for Japheth's sake, but now for their own. Shem's beautiful wife, Asenath, is very quiet and dignified, while Ham's Junia is just the opposite. Junia is irrepressible naturally, but even she is sobered by these transcendent events. Noah's wife, Lydia, is most beautiful of all. I think Japheth looks like his mother. And Noah has indeed been a loving father to me. I married his favorite son and that partly accounts for his fondness for me.

After the sun went down, showing but dimly through the mist, we rose and prepared for watching the skies and other outward portents betokening the coming Deluge. The tremendous tragedy overshadowing our own lives rendered us all silent. The moon was at its full. An increasing light in the east gave token of its approach. "The Flood-tide," said the Prophet, "will soon be upon us. Even if the Devas should now return and attempt the removal of their retinues in waiting at Balonia it could not be accomplished. They would be met on every side by the advancing waters and their overthrow hastened. They must renounce forever now their assumed bodies of flesh and return to their normal condition to be bound in fetters by the Almighty. Their giant sons they will see no more. In a few hours the Deluge will inevitably reach us; but fear not, my children; let your faith in God be manifested in the midst of the very terrors that surround us; they are but the fulfillment of His immutable word."

Silently, with eyes and ears strained to catch every portent of what was about to come, we sat by the window and watched the blood-stained moon slowly mount the heavens; for in the ominous silence we knew an implacable sentry held ward, one that the bravest can scarcely meet without dread—Azelles, the Angel of Death!

The Hour of Doom

Soon after midnight we heard a sound in the air like a shriek, or wail, passing over the valley. Afterward came short sudden gusts, succeeded by hollow intervals of intense calm. Breathless we listened. The Spirits of the Air seemed to be in distress. There were voices in complaint—moaning, angry yelling. A sullen, far-off roar caused the earth to tremble. I covered my head to shut out all sense and compel oblivion. In vain! As faint dawn glimmered feebly in the East, a heavy blast swirled down from the North with a force that shook our building and chilled us to the bone. In a few moments came a hot wind from the opposite direction; the air was filled with dust and at the same time an unusual dampness was felt.

Hoping that this awful event would not come to pass was not possible. "O, Japheth," I cried, "Azelles and the Prince of the Power of the Air rage in darkness above the valley and the earth shudders!" We rose hastily and all stood in silence with bowed heads and faces covered.

We then approached the broad window; and glanced upward we shrank back terrified from what we saw in the sky. Around the cramped, distorted horizon a lurid haze had settled. Over this crawled a great mass of brownish vapor and high above was a dome of black clouds, like great rocks rolling in the skies.

Yet no wind now stirred the leaves; a painful, awful stillness brooded over all. The city was aroused. Housetop and towers became crowded with men gazing at the portentous heavens. Suddenly, as by a common impulse, all eyes were turned to the North, where had come but shortly before the cold blast and terrible shudder.

O sight of horror, before which even the heart of the boldest Deva must quail! Entirely across the entrance of the valley, crowding the very mountaintops, appeared a mighty wall, tottering, crashing, falling, pressed forward by some invisible power. Upon its awful front, in confusion which dazed the sight, were borne timbers, fragments of buildings, earth, rocks and mutilated bodies of animals and creatures of the sea. But most dreadful of all, tossed in uncertain motion, were the ghastly corpses of dead men and women and children.

Beyond and above, heaped against the lowering sky, were seen oncoming cold, angry seas, raging breakers, monster water-spouts, clutching the clouds and roaring as if all the waters of the world were dashed together in a frenzy of destruction. With piercing shrieks the crowds turned to flee, but look! another horror—another flood hung above the city, borne onward from the South—the Oceans of Death were closing above the valley. Paralyzed with fear and despair, all stood motionless, until a cry arose—

"To the hills, to the hills!" Then up the rocky steep they rushed—strong men and Darvands, delicate women, confused children, panic-stricken by the fear of imminent death. As the mass pressed madly on, many were dashed over the rocks and fell shrieking into the gulf below.

Strange power of the human mind! Amid the wild unreality of that tremendous scene, as in a picture surrounded by most terrible accessories, I saw and recognized in the flying crowd some of the attendants of the Palace and other royal households. One group impressed itself as vividly as the lightning flash that revealed it—a beautiful woman (her dress a queen's) with an infant pressed to her bosom, while by the hand she led a child whose, strong features and powerful limbs too surely betrayed a celestial parentage. Her hair and garments streamed in the wind, which she vainly strove to manage, and her voice of despair sounded shrill above the roar of the storm—"Save us, O Owadu, save us!"

Far from the reach of her voice, in chains of darkness, was Owadu, the Deva, her husband, awaiting the Judgment of the Last Day!

In another instant all sense and feeling were absorbed in the jarring shock that we ourselves experienced. The floods rushed together, sky and ocean mingled, the writhing vapors were torn by a mighty force, the floodgates of heaven were opened and an inundation from the clouds swelled the wild waters already surging through the valley. The sharp lightning flashes split the heavy vault, the thick air was whirled into a tornado, the winds shrieked and howled like infuriated demons, twisting and tearing everything in their course. To increase the horrible distraction and noise, immense flocks of birds and bats of every description were hurtled through the darkening air into the greedy wave, despite helpless screams and violent flutterings.

And now approached the unimaginable horror. An earthquake, of awful violence, rocked the valley, one moment stretching it out like a plane, tossing the wreckage to the very heavens and the next sinking so deep that the mountain-tops seemed about to topple over and crush us. The mighty billows in quick succession roared above the hills and shortly settled into a cloud of inky blackness. A fierce antagonism of fire and flood ensued, the ribs of earth were cracked, its crust was ripped opened, subterranean fires belched forth and a terrible eruption of hissing water and melted rock, with chaos and darkness, shut us in.

The avalanche hung over us for a quick breath and then descended. Above the howling of the storm, the roaring waters and bellowing earthquake, an awful crash was heard. The vessel staggered, heaved and spun around in the boiling whirlpool like a dry leaf in the wind. O that horrible sickening swirl!

Dizzy and stunned, we fell prostrate, the color left our faces, the warm current of life was frozen, our hearts almost ceased to beat; we were within the jaws of death, we sank into an abyss! O God, shield us and protect us from this fearful hour! was the cry of each heart.

Then the Tebah made a tremendous lurch, plunged completely under water, trembled in every joint, righted again and crashing through a thousand wrecks, came up unharmed.

"God be praised!" exclaimed our father Noah, "we are afloat!"

And with pale, earnest lips we all echoed, "God be praised!"

Peril and Gloom

The torrents of destruction were yet contending for mastery over us. At one time we thought that the waters from the North would prevail and drive us almost upon the remaining towers of the city. Again we were dashed back the length of the valley by the torrent from the South. Entangled among wrecks which covered the mighty surge, the timbers of our staunch vessel groaned and creaked as if they would part. We could feel the commotion from beneath as we were helplessly dragged across rocks, tree-tops and submerged buildings.

But our Ark of shelter was planned by a Divine Architect, even by Him who sent the Deluge, for He knew it would be required in this hour of unequaled peril. Our great boat lived in a boiling, tempestuous sea where the stateliest ship would have been shattered to fragments.

After many days of convulsive turmoil, the storm somewhat subsided though the waters still rose rapidly along the hillsides. We breathed more freely and our father Noah looked after the frightened beasts, from whom we had heard occasional moans of pain and fear. At length, with half averted gaze, we ventured to gain approach to the window. O vision of gloom! The heavens were gathering blackness and heavy masses of cloud were driving across the murky sky. The pale moon was drowned in a black, watery mist; its feeble sickly light revealed the dim outlines of the horror by which we were surrounded. We were drifting near a mountain of unfamiliar outline, whose top was crowded with living beings in every attitude and aspect of despair. Women and children were gone. Their feeble natures had yielded long before this terrible consummation. But men and Darvands, animals, birds, serpents, were all crowded in indistinguishable confusion. Some sat in motionless apathy, with despairing faces upturned to the gloomy sky. Some with frantic cries and outstretched arms wildly implored our aid, others with insane laughter sprang into the awful waters, in desperate attempts to reach our vessel.

But shrieks of terror, strangled cries of the dying and the howl of beasts, were in an instant hushed, as the dense darkness suddenly swallowed all! And now a terrific storm again burst forth in renewed fury. Heaven and earth were shaken by fearful bursts of thunder; incessant and awful flashes of lightning illumined the night. Rain came down in torrents! Before this dreadful time, the earth had known no rain; therefore the incredulous had paid no heed to Noah's repeated warnings of the coming deluge. And now it appeared as though windows were opened in heaven and the flood poured forth with relentless fury. To the poor people perishing in the flood, the sight of so much rain descending from the heavens seemed most strange and terrible.

We could hear the swollen breakers roaring over the mountain-steeps. Feeble daylight at length struggled faintly through the enveloping shroud of darkness and we could see many dead bodies floating all around us; later, thicker darkness shut us in. Our noble father Noah was a pillar of strength to us all through these dark days and cheered and comforted us in our deep distress. Who can describe the anguish caused by witnessing the desolation of a world! Yet we preserved a measure of tranquillity, even in the midst of universal destruction, knowing that this was but a just retribution permitted by the All-Powerful One as a lasting example of the results of disobedience.

Again and again did day blacken into night of only a deeper shade of blackness. Then the long night would pale into a semblance of day. We would welcome even the faintest rays of light and eagerly awaited the cessation of the tempest.

Finally, the Prophet spoke to us in words of comfort: "My dear ones, God Almighty, the All-Powerful One, has preserved us from the ravaging floods when we were utterly helpless. Forever blessed be His name! He will always be mindful of the obedient. He has chosen us out of all the world, unworthy though we are, to continue the human race. Now we have come through this great flood and remain alive, let us now partake of food that our strength may revive for I perceive that you all look pale and weary from want of food and sleep. Later my good wife will prepare you a soothing drink of herb leaves which will induce sleep."

Accordingly we ate food and partook of the warm drinks, then retired for a much needed rest. My head barely touched the pillow of my couch when I was lost in a profound slumber, too deep to admit of dreams. When I awakened I was surprised to find that the water had become comparatively calm. We seemed to have settled into a sheltered place, where we were not shaken by billows and winds.

Our life within our marvelous Tebah now began to be conducted in a more orderly fashion. Every one went about his or her duties more cheerfully, with a sense of deep gratitude for so great a deliverance. Each tried to make the other happy and I learned that Noah's sons were resourceful men, adept in many arts and sciences acquired from their ancestors.

My love of study was now somewhat gratified. The family of Noah possessed many rare and wonderful manuscripts containing histories of former events. From these I eagerly selected one written by Enoch before his Translation. It appeared from this that Enoch was only three hundred years old when our first father Adam died and had heard from Adam's own lips of all that happened from Creation down to his own day. In reading this valued manuscript I shed many tears over the account of the entrance of sin into our world. How little did our mother Eve realize what her beloved children would suffer for her thoughtless deed. I was reading this account when Japheth entered and finding me in tears gently inquired the cause and was relieved to find that they were induced by an ancient sorrow.

THE CORONAL OF HESPERUS

The rain descends incessantly. A black mist enshrouds the horizon. Yesterday our little family assembled in our mother's apartment and I read from the writings of Allimades a story of olden times: "The Love of Endymion, a Star-spirit, for Offobia, Princess of the Kingdom of Nourma." We were all much affected by the great trials and virtue of the princess, unshaken even to her very end, when the gate of death closed upon her fair form and Endymion could see her no more.

This story was a gift from my father when I was but a child. Often had I retired to the recesses of the forest to linger over the scroll and dream undisturbed of the fortunes of Orrobia. How mysterious then seemed the love of a Star-spirit for a mortal maiden! And now is the mystery solved? No! The sadness of my heart increased and fearing some word or look might betray it, I presently withdrew to the solitude of my own chamber. Here I looked once more upon the memorials of my former life—the treasures and parchments of Allimades, the shawl and robe wrought by Samoula's hand and the rare utensils, Minerva's dying gift.

The bodies of these, my loved ones, now lie beneath the mighty waves. In death they will sleep their long sleep—perchance many centuries until the awakening time and Paradise is restored on earth. All except the repentant Deva, Hesperus. Ah, Hesperus!—though now chained with other fallen angels, in the distant future, when your Day of final Judgment has come, you will come forth purified, restored, forgiven!

My eyes fell upon the jewel-chest, his gift, which poor Aldeth had conveyed from the Palace—the last service of her devoted life, who also now sleeps beneath the heaving billows. The chest has never been opened. I might now look upon its contents. With trembling fingers I pressed the spring. It unclosed; a soft perfume was exhaled and a light vapor passed from an ivory tablet which bore these words:

Sigh with me, Aloma,
Answer sigh by sigh;
Drink with me, Aloma,
The cup of ecstasy.

Love with me, Aloma,
Then shall bliss unknown,
Born of angel's passion
Ever be thine own.

I raised the tablet, and beneath, upon a silken cushion, lay a diadem of rarest beauty—a wreath of silver lilies, exquisitely wrought and frosted snowy white. Depending from the slender filaments were quivering pearls and deep in the heart of each delicate flower an opal flowed like smothered fire. Ah, Hesperus!

Tears dropped from my eyes upon the precious garland. I hear the footsteps of my husband. Why do I fear that he will find me weeping!

He looks upon my grief with sad surprise, discovers the chest, divines the cause of my tears, reverently takes the glistening crown from its resting place, and places it upon my forehead, saying, "Aloma, my queen!"

After a few moments of thoughtful silence my husband spoke again—"Beloved, your life before the happy hour when first we met is to me unknown." I comprehended his reasonable desire and without reserve confided to him my strange history, at which he marveled greatly and forgave my tears, embraced me tenderly and in return for such confidence related many wonderful events of his own life, the adventures he had, and how he was at various times wonderfully delivered by the power of God from failing into the power of the wicked Star-spirits and the powerful and treacherous Darvands, their giant sons.

The Tide Turns

Evening

It is now the forty-eighth day since we entered the Tebah. Several remarkable things occurred yesterday. Early in the morning I was awakened by a shaft of sunlight streaming into my chamber through the window. Its brilliance was dazzling. I had never beheld anything so bright and wonderful before.

What strange phenomenon is this? I thought within myself as I ran to the window and awestruck beheld the sun rising in the East, a huge ball of golden fire tinging all the sky around it with waves of vivid color. I was lost in admiration and wonder.

What had happened? It had ceased raining and the sun was unveiled for the first time to human eyes. Vaguely at first I comprehended the significance of the sun's new glory. Until this time the sun had been veiled by this watery ring which had now descended. The waves were still rippling toward the Tebah and were all tinged with gold reflecting the radiance of the sun.

Were the others aware of this new beauty? Quickly robing I ran to the general room where the family was going to meet. I found all gathered together and after exchanging morning greetings learned that my experience had been shared by all. We then joined in reverent prayer of praise and thanksgiving, led as usual by the honored head of the family.

Shem retired to his own quarters and inspired by this event composed a sacred song expressing our joy over this occurrence.Then he joined us and with beaming face chanted it for our benefit, accompanying it with the soft tones of the harp. Everything now took on a new air of cheerfulness and everybody went about their daily occupations with the new song on their lips.

I slowly became aware, at first refusing to credit my observations, that Ham did not seem to join in our devotions as heartily as the rest. His careless remarks and lack of family respect often causes his father and mother to display an anxious expression which they endeavor to hide from all.

We all eagerly awaited the appearing of the moon and stars in the evening, being informed by Noah that they would present a spectacle equally wonderful to the rising of the sun. Nor were we disappointed in our expectations, for pale but serenely beautiful appeared the moon slowly ascending from the horizon, the tranquil waters reflecting the golden glow. In the blue vault of heaven the stars began to make their appearance in bewildering number and varied beauty. We watched them in fascinated silence.

At length Noah spoke and said, "Hear what I have to say: the God of all flesh has revealed to my forefathers that this mighty deluge marks a great epoch in the history of the world, to be succeeded by other ages, in which Satanas will endeavor to outwit the Almighty and will apparently succeed, only to be completely vanquished in the end by a mighty one who will come in the name of the Lord. May His gracious will be accomplished and may we, His children, abide faithful and awake to behold the Paradise that was lost by our first parents Adam and Eve."

Many other things did Noah relate to us, too many to record here, but suddenly Japheth, who had been watching the waters, exclaimed: "The waters are receding." This discovery was soon confirmed by all. We began to wonder how long we would yet be confined in our Tebah.

AZELLES

This evening I stood alone and watched the waves, as in capricious play with the wind they rippled against the sides of our vessel. Twilight brooded over the boundless ocean—a sea with no cities on its shores, no islands, no ships plowing its waves, nor birds skimming the surface, only infinite tranquillity and silence—and the night. The Tebah drifted in the soft breeze, the darkness deepened and a shadow fell upon my soul as memory recalled the past.

It was but a short time, and yet it seemed an age, since I listened to the wind in the cypress-tops and to the sound of the river flowing on, calm as the current of my life. Ah, what unexpected depths of passion, what strange events awaited me! Only He who can read the secrets of the hearts knows the struggle, the difficulties through which He has permitted me to pass. With no human guide to direct, no one to understand but He who is the Father of the fatherless. A nameless melancholy fills my heart.

Upon a rock projecting from the water stood motionless a tall figure enshrouded in black robes, leaning upon a heavy sword, and as we floated near, I recognized the dread form of Azelles, the Dark Angel! His eye swept over the waste of waters and I heard these words:

"The work is finished, the decrees of the Most High are fulfilled and I go to Him from whom I came."

As he was saying this he loosened his black cowl and mantle and cast them with his sword into the sea; for the insignia of pain and woe are not permitted to enter the realm of Heaven.

As he soared upward, there was revealed a form so ineffably fair, a face so radiant with eternal youth, that in sudden surprise, not conscious of my words, I murmured: "O beautiful angel, no longer disguised, I see you as an angel of Life! Do not leave me so soon. I would partake of your life!"

At this moment a hand was laid on my shoulder and a voice spoke softly, "Are you dreaming, Aloma?" I turned toward the speaker and my eyes met those of Japheth. His arms enfolded me and the vision vanished.

Aloma Foretells the Glory of the Japhetic Tribes

Fourth Moon.

Since the night of the departure of Azelles from the earth, Japheth seldom leaves me alone. He did not see the angel, but my words alarmed him; and so it happened that when I came this evening to enjoy the sunset he came also and sat by my side.

We never tire of watching the sun sink into the waste of waters, transforming the heavens to a mass of glorious color, gradually fading to paler shades and fainter glow until the last ray disappears.

Japheth broke the eloquent silence (I have found one can be silent with those they love) with the words: "Aloma, I have a peculiar love for the setting sun. I have often wondered what land it looks upon as it passes from our sight. In the West there is some attraction which I cannot resist; my eyes turn there and my heart follows. Does it not seem strange to you, my beloved?"

"Japheth," I answered, "I understand; the same impulse impels me, even at this moment!"

With my face blushing I spoke. "An Illumination from the Holy One comes to me. I can pierce the cloud of the future and see the majestic but awful pageant of human life move down the path of time—onward, resting never, merged in the ocean of Infinity!

"The sons of Japheth are a little band; the band increases to a tribe, the tribe becomes mighty nations. Like a whirlwind they sweep toward the West. Their sons are mighty warriors. None more fair than the daughters of Japheth. I hear the noise of battle, the thunder of engines of war! Javan and Tubal emblazoned on hostile banners. I regret that sons of mine should meet in mortal combat. Still the power of the serpent prevails, setting brother against brother. The children of Javan obtain universal control—another mighty conflict and Elam arises to rule the world. Again the world is drenched in blood, a people of a small country but mighty in deeds of war wrench the dominion from the children of Shem.

"Cities arise in the wilderness! Waste places bloom like a garden. Multitudes fill the earth and subdue it.

"Westward still press the sons of Japheth; where the bright sun leads they follow. I see floating palaces like our Tebah upon the stormy seas; they depend not upon the wind but move by a power within themselves. They send messages at the speed as the lightning. Upon the land are chariots of iron and wood which go—swiftly but smoothly along the highways. There are ships that fly like birds through the air.

I hear the thunder of the nations as they clamor for freedom from the oppressive yokes of kings and rulers. They endeavor wholly free, every man a king as Adam before he sinned. In impotent anger they kill one line of oppressors only to come under the rule of another. They are most to be pitied! But wait, I see that deliverance comes at last, though not by human beings. He who created our first parent comes to the rescue. More than this is yet hidden from my view."

My eyes closed and as I sank away overpowered by the wonderful vision, Japheth caught me in his arms, exclaiming: "Come back to me, Aloma, I cannot live without you!" My strength returned and he continued: "Dark are your words; I do not understand what your saying. Let us leave the future to unravel its own mysteries while we live and love in the present."

So present happiness occupied our words and thoughts. Yet strangely contrasting with our tranquil joy, suggested, perhaps by the vision which pictured our children at enmity among themselves, Lamech's sad poem runs through my head:

"Adah and Zillah I hear my voice,
Ye wives of Lamech! I give ear unto my speech;
For a man had I slain for smiting me,
And a youth for wounding me:
Surely sevenfold shall Cain be avenged,
But Lamech seventy and seven."

Too bad that we should pass on this sad heritage to our children. O Adversary of our race, how long will you prevail to plant seeds of hatred in the hearts of the children of men?

The Tebah Touches Land

Seventh Month—Seventeenth Day

At daybreak this morning we were awakened by a sudden jarring of the Tebah, which threw my couch against the wall. Awakening so abruptly from a deep, dreamless sleep, it required a breathing space or two to realize what had happened. Then I understood instinctively that the Tebah was fast aground.

With much less than the usual time devoted to getting dressed, I was ready. The musical but subdued tones of the harp summoned the family to morning worship. I ran to the central chamber. Only Noah and Lydia were there.

Noah was at the hearth replenishing the fire, which had almost gone out. It soon began to blaze cheerfully. I reclined on a cushion at Lydia's feet as we discussed the momentous occurrence.

"Dear child," said Lydia, "This is indeed a day never to be forgotten. At last we have reached our goal. The peril of the deep no longer threatens. We are safe on land again and it is now only a question of days perhaps where we may emerge from our temporary refuge and dwell once more on our native earth.

"We do not know where we are except it was revealed to Noah before we embarked on this long voyage that we would anchor on a mountain in the center of the world. God has guarded us all in our journey."

When the family were all present we engaged in our accustomed morning prayer with joyful and thankful solemnity.

Land Appears

Tenth Month—First Day.

It is now two months and thirteen days since we rested on earth. A constant watch has been kept to discern the first appearance of land. All are beginning to feel their confinement now. All longed for the day of release. We tried in vain to picture the earth as it would now appear. Would we be able to recognize the old ruins? Or would the face of the earth be so changed that we would find no familiar landmarks? We could only surmise and wait.

At last the happy day arrived. Our brother Ham first discerned the welcome sight of land. It was a small black object rising from the vast sea. Slowly did the waters sink, slowly the mountain peak emerged. Now even the animals became restless. It had been my daily habit to feed the sheep and other small animals, a duty I had grown to enjoy, and I had made friends with many of them. Japheth promised me that the little lamb born during the voyage should be mine. Poor animals; they will be glad too, to have their freedom again.

Eleventh Month—Tenth Day.

This morning Noah opened the window of the Tebah and sent forth a raven but it returned in the evening to the Tebah. The waters are gradually receding. Much of the surrounding country is now visible. We can only discern that the mountain on which we have rested is very high and descends to the valley below by gentle slopes. This will enable us to leave the Tebah without difficulty. Ham can barely be restrained from endeavoring to go forth now but Noah has persuaded him that the Most High has provided him with a sign by which he will recognize the proper time.

Eleventh Month-Twenty-fourth Day.

Seven days since Noah opened the window and sent forth a dove. Away she flew and was soon lost to sight. In the evening she returned and Noah put forth his hand and caught her and brought her in. He waited again seven days and sent forth the dove a second time. In the evening she returned as before but in her beak was a fresh olive-leaf! He now summoned the family to relate to us this memorable incident. The waters are abated from off the earth.

First Month—First Day.

There came a day when our little dove rever returned and we saw her no more.

Today Noah with his three sons removed the covering of the ark and we beheld a beautiful scene. There were mountains stretching in every direction and valleys with glistening rivers traversing them. The sky above was a beautiful blue. All nature seemed to present a joyous aspect. I gave myself up to the rapturous enjoyment of this magnificent sight.

There are now no wicked Devas to again destroy the human race. How strange to think there is not a sound of living beings in all the world but within the narrow confines of our Tebah. This universal silence will never again prevail, a brooding silence while nature meditates a new beginning. The old world has ended, the new begun! What yet undreamed of possibilities are reserved for our race?

Third Month—Fourth Day.

Arguri. On the slopes of Ararat.

It is seven days since we left the Tebah. On that day God spoke to Noah and commanded him to go forth, he, his wife and children, and take with him every living thing that was with him in the Tebah. This commandment Noah swiftly obeyed. The camels, elephants and horses bore the heavier burdens as we unloaded the Tebah. The Tebah appeared desolate, indeed deserted by its occupants.

Noah led the procession, the family following. Slowly we descended the mountain. The animals went cautiously at first, being timid, but soon acquired confidence and scattered in every direction—all except the animals which bore our possessions and domestic cattle and fowl, which continued to follow us down the mountain.

THE RAINBOW PLEDGE

For several hours we journeyed and halted at noon. Our father Noah built an altar unto the Lord and sacrificed some of the clean cattle and fowl upon the altar. All gathered around the altar as the Prophet lifted his eyes to heaven and offered thanks to the Almighty for our preservation. And the Lord was pleased with the sacrifice and drew near and communed with the Prophet.

The Lord spoke and said: "I establish my covenant with you; and all flesh, and with your seed after you; and all flesh shall not be cut off any more by the waters of a flood. This is the token of the covenant which I make between me and you and every living creature that is with you for perpetual generations. My bow I do set in the cloud and it shall be for a token of the covenant between me and the earth."

Simultaneously with the words of the Lord appeared the rainbow in the sky, composed of all the colors, and very beautiful to behold.

Noah's Intoxication

Seventh Month—First Day

A strange and sad thing happened to our beloved Father. I hardly know how to record it. Noah being a farmer had preserved seeds of all plants in the Tebah, and on settling on the slope of this mountain, he and his sons tilled the ground and planted the seeds. Noah invented a very useful instrument for this purpose called a plow and by means of this their labor was much lessened.

When the grapes were ripe Lydia made from their juice a wine and gave to Noah to drink as he returned from harvest one day much wearied, thinking it would refresh him. But it had a strange and unusual effect upon him. He became intoxicated, and Ham, entering the tent of his father, found him—uncovered! Hard-hearted as he did not care for his father's predicament but hastened to his brothers and recounted it to them. Shem's indignation at his brother Ham's unrighteous conduct knew no bounds. Shem and Japheth then ran to the assistance of their father, and entering the tent backwards covered their father with a garment.

At length Noah awakened from his sleep and was informed about what had happened. His marvelous mind quickly grasped the significance of this startling event. He instructed his sons that a new thing had happened. The juice of the grape had fermented. This had been impossible before the Deluge. But the climate was greatly altered after the flood, causing food to ferment and spoil very rapidly.

Shem and Japheth were blessed by their father for their good deed; but regarding Ham, Noah said that his descendants would be servants.

* * * *

Here the manuscript abruptly ended, but upon the back of the linen roll was an inscription in bolder characters, which after careful study we found to be—

The Story of Javan

After the Flood, 500 Years

Aloma, our honored and loving mother, has left us. She sleeps in the land of Ararat, in the land of forgetfulness, where all our fathers have journeyed, and where all the living must follow. Seven days ago she called me to her side and said:

"My dear Javan, it seems not possible that it is now five hundred years since the Deluge! How rapidly the years have slipped by! I was just emerging from childhood at that time. How gracious the Lord has been in bestowing on me seven noble sons. May the All-Beneficent One guard your future.

"In times past I was permitted by the Almighty God to have a vision of the future. In that vision I beheld the attempt of the mighty Satanas, who together with his cohorts was restrained in darkness at the time of the Deluge, that they might no longer appear in human form."

My mother ceased speaking for some moments; her thoughts seemed far away. At length she resumed:

"As on that night do I seem to hear the voice of Japheth crying to me, 'Aloma, Aloma, my beloved!"

"Dear Japheth, I come!—not to the shelter of the perishable Tebah, but to rest with you in peaceful sleep in the dust of the earth until that happy day when we shall be awakened and enjoy forever the restored Paradise of God.

"And now I must depart. To you, O Javan, in whose arms it was foretold I should die, I commit the keeping of this journal, which faithfully I have kept according to the words of Allimades. This I entrust to your care for the benefit of my posterity, who are now scattered throughout the earth. Once they spoke a single language, but because of their disobedience in building the Tower of Babel, their languages were confused and they were scattered to the four corners of the earth. In vain did I warn them to desist from their impious course in building that Tower. You remember my grief at their refusal to heed my warning. But a mother's love cannot die. Let my wealth be equally divided among them, and convey to them my blessing.

"The history of the great Deluge has been transmitted by other survivors of our family. My record agrees with theirs. When you lay me in the tomb beside the dust of your father place in my hand the amethyst cylinder brought from the library of Allimades and let it contain this record."

Here my mother motioned all in attendance to retire, which we did, borne down with grief at her approaching death.

In the night there was a commotion in the royal pavilion. The attendants of my mother were summoned. Hastily I entered the chamber and raised my mother in my arms. Her life was rapidly departing. Once more the old prophetic fire flashed from her eyes and wondrous words came from her quivering lips:

"Again I have a vision of the future. I behold coming to the earth the promised seed of the woman, born from a favored one, a descendant of our kinsman Abraham. This marks the opening of the Divine purpose effecting the deliverance of our family and not ours only, but all the families of the earth.

"He is the Messenger of the Lord. He announces that he comes not to do his own will but the will of his Father, who sent him. He is the chief of all creation. He is the Right Hand of Almighty God. In some marvelous way, which is not now revealed, he causes the sentence passed upon our father Adam to be satisfied, that Adam and his race may be released. I behold that he dies as a man and is raised out of death a powerful, glorious being and elevated to the highest position in the universe next to God. I see written the words that he came to destroy Satanas and his works, and that Satanas shall be destroyed.

"The scene changes. Century rolls on after century. Dimly I see a wonderful work progressing in silent grandeur, unknown and unnoticed by mankind.

"At last the mighty Prince appears again. Now he comes in power and great glory and proceeds at once with the work appointed for him, to overthrow and destroy the power of Satanas the usurper. There is great commotion on the earth and all the nations are in distress and perplexity. Wars, pestilences and famines afflict the peoples of all lands. Selfish men, goaded on by Satanas, plunge the world into a terrible time of trouble which becomes so intense that it mounts to the very heavens, and the hearts of men are melted because of the trouble. The world reels to and fro and staggers like one who is drunk, and men are at their wits' end. They cry unto the Almighty in their trouble and He helps them out of their distress. He makes the storm calm, so that the waves thereof are still. And then stands forth the Prince of Peace and commands the storms to subside, and sweet peace settles down upon the earth.

'I see poor, depraved humanity, so long fettered by the power of Satanas and the fallen angels, being gradually lifted up out of their degradation and freed from their darkness. All the chains of ignorance, superstition are broken. Satanas and his associates are stripped of all power. I see the mighty hosts returning from the prison house of death and being brought again to their own land. They come with rejoicing. The tender ties of home and family, broken by death, are re-established. My mother, too, shall stand in her lot at the end of the days and be reunited to her beloved ones.

'I behold Allimades with Samoula by his side. There is also Minerva, Aldeth and Cheros in the bloom of youth. These, with joyful song, walk with each other beneath the trees by the beautiful streams of water; the birds are singing, the trees are clapping their hands for joy; and all creation is singing the praise of Jehovah.

"Hesperus, too, I see once more in beauty, having been restored to harmony with the great Creator. He rejoices at my awakening. With pleasure he speaks: "Aloma, welcome to the kingdom of Messiah. Obey the great King of kings and Lord of lords and your life shall be endless and unlimited joy your portion." I see a host of angels in heaven, who respond: 'Joy to you, Hesperus, you who have loved the light.'

"I see the beauty and glory of Eden restored. The deserts are blossoming as the rose; the whole earth yields its increase and is made as the Garden of Eden. There follows a government which satisfies the desires of all honest men. The people sow the fields and plant vineyards which yield abundantly. Wars are forgotten, sickness is no more; there is not even a fear of such things. I behold a restored earth, a restored people. Sorrow has passed away. There is no more crying, no more tears. There is no more death. I see a host of angels in heaven praising God. I behold a host in the earth catching up their songs and joining in the praise until everything that breathes is singing the praise of Jehovah and his beloved Son, the Prince of Peace.

"The vision of Aloma is ended!"

Here the voice of my mother, which had been so marvelously sustained, failed her. Utterly exhausted by this last supreme effort, she sank rapidly. She seemed to be almost gone. Thus she lay for half an hour.

Then her large, luminous eyes opened once more. She raised her finger and seemed to be listening. Then she whispered softly:

"Hush! the sound of the river coming, coming—Eternal Life! Eternal Harmony!"

In another moment with a radiant smile the eager, earnest eyes closed forever. Aloma was dead.

My mother was buried beside our father in the tomb on the mountain of Ararat. On her brow was set the crown her humility had declined, and "The Journal," encased in imperishable crystal, will be placed in her hand, perchance for the benefit of future ages, when the wonderful events of her life, recorded therein, may have passed from the memory of man. Upon the walls of her tomb have we sculptured the Arbor-Vitae, emblem of that which she saw in dying vision; and when the shadows of death gather over us, may we also apprehend its significance, and with the latest breath bless the God of Japheth and Aloma.

The words of Javan are ended.

0-595-00516-0

CPSIA information can be obtained at www.ICGtesting.com
Printed in the USA
LVOW061319190712

290748LV00001B/14/A